Thirty and single? Well, getcha ass to the Gathering!

Whitney Wickham is at the darned annual werewolf Gathering all right. Only there's one problem: she doesn't belong there. Her sisters carry the Mark indicating they'll mate an Alpha Pair of wolves, while Whitney does not have that lovely, swirling scar. She's been hauled half way around the world to be stared at, and not-so-covertly sniffed, for no reason. Unfortunately the gorgeous, drool worthy, magic-mojo-wielding Wardens don't know why she's been summoned to the Gathering any more than she does. Which sucks. But at least they're hot.

Emmett Greene and Levy Walters are Wardens—keepers of the law and embodiment of the magic of the werewolves. They can never mate, never marry, and never form a lasting romantic relationship. It's a hard and fast law that keeps their powers pure of outside influence.

Rules are going to be broken.

One look at Whitney, one hint of her scent, and they realize their immovable laws might have to jiggle. She's got luscious curves, a wicked smile, and a mouth that would make a thousand men weep. No matter the rules, their inner wolves will claim her. The only things standing in their way are the Elder Wardens who will do anything… anything… to keep Emmett and Levy from discovering the truth: the laws are wrong. And being with Whitney Wickham is so very, very right.

Chapter One

Whitney reminded herself that she was not a violent person. She had to recall she was sweetness and light and everything bright. Hell, she helped old ladies cross the road, went to church on Sundays, and donated to charity every Christmas and Easter. She was a good person, damn it.

She definitely wasn't the type of woman who dreamt of stabbing the Gathering organizer in the eye with a pen. Pens he, of course, ordered for the attendees to use as desired. Then again, maybe she did dream of that since she couldn't wait to see one protruding from the werewolf's eye socket. That's what *she* desired. She snatched one from the table and gripped the thin piece of plastic. *Nothing like being prepared.*

The Ruling Wardens, the werewolves who also wielded the magic of the wolves and upheld the laws for all of North America, were avoiding her and she was about done. She'd been at the Gathering since Friday afternoon and it was now late Sunday morning. The men weren't anywhere in sight. She wasn't normally this bitchy, but enough was enough. A gal could only enjoy the spa at the werewolf run hotel so much before she was ready to pull her perfectly styled hair out.

"So, tell me again when I'll get to see the Wardens?" Whitney managed to shove the words past her gritted teeth. It was the wolves' fault. Ever since she'd arrived at the Gathering, her timid, sweet exterior had transformed into raging "kill people" mode.

1

The man trembled and she didn't kid herself it was due to her. Nope, the Ruling Wardens were scary guys. Well, as far as the wolves were concerned. The Ruling Alphas held their position through dominance and brute force, things other wolves understood. Even their beasts recognized the situation with ease. It was instinctual, animalistic, feral. That said, the Ruling Wardens kept their position through magic alone. The two of them had so much power there wasn't another in the world who'd would ever think of challenging them. For the Ruling Wardens, death could come with a thought.

"W-W-Well, the Ruling Wardens are meeting with the wolves with legitimate concerns and they said—"

"Legitimate…" She took a deep, calming breath and stared at the far wall.

The hallway echoed with people—wolves and humans alike—heading to meetings. Hotel staff darted between bodies on two feet and stumbled past the few who wandered around on four. Apparently, being in wolf form made the whole sniffy speed dating thing easier. Soon they'd be going into the second round of Tests of Proximity of the day. There, Alpha Pairs got to sit around and see if any of the Marked females belong to them. Sniff! Mark tingles! Mate!

Voices bounced off the pale marble tile, and the sun shining through the massive floor-to-ceiling windows illuminated luxurious decorations. Hotel Garou was the premier place for wolf-y vacation as well as the location of the annual Gathering. Apparently mate-finding needed to happen in the lap of luxury.

She needed to see the Ruling Wardens. Now. Today. They were responsible for creating the magic that delivered the Gathering summons to her home. Now they needed to get their mojo working on why *she'd* been ordered to attend. Hopefully before the Gathering wrapped up shop for the year.

The Gathering was meant to be a big ol' party where those who carried a Mark could mingle with Alpha Pairs and hopefully find their mates. Of course, if a Marked wasn't mated by age thirty, their attendance was required. The Wickham triplets had hit thirty and here they were. Not showing up resulted in… something. She still wasn't clear on what would have happened if the Wickham gals had stayed home.

The problem Whitney faced was that while the first two of the Wickham triplets, Scarlet and Gabriella, carried a Mark, she did not. She'd checked. Hell, her sisters had even looked in those hard to reach places. There was no flesh-colored, scar-like symbol on her body indicating she'd someday mate two werewolves and live happily ever after.

There would be no "woo hoo, cue the rice tossing and tie a few cans to the bumper of their car" for Whitney Wickham. She wasn't bitter. Not much, anyway.

She wanted that happy ending, damn it, but she couldn't have it until the Wardens figured out where their mojo went wrong. Hell, for all she knew there were wires crossed inside her and that's why she'd been summoned. That was probably the reason she hadn't ever been happy with any of her exes. It was like bits and pieces of her were Marked while the rest wasn't. The "want to" was there but the "screw you, it'll never happen" was a little too strong. Could that be her problem?

She didn't know the answer to that question because the freaking Ruling Wardens were dealing with *legitimate* concerns.

3

"Look, furball. I'm the Ruling Alpha Mate's sister and—"

"You aren't a wolf nor a Marked. The Ruling Wardens are resolving wolf matters." The organizer growled, his eyes flashing yellow and he curled his lip.

Oh heck no, she wasn't about to be intimidated. Gripping the pen even tighter, she raised her hand, ready to stab the wolf. She been hauled halfway around the world and had spent the last two days simply waiting for the Wardens to arrive. They'd dragged their asses and now she didn't have a *legitimate* concern. She'd show him legitimate.

Whitney growled, ready to poke tiny holes into the man, only to have her fun snatched from her. Literally.

"No stabbing ma peeps, Whit. If I hafta be nice to 'em, so do you." Her sister Scarlet plucked the pen from her hand and then gave the organizer her attention, popping him on the nose with it as if he were a wayward puppy. "Callum, she pulled the 'Kickass Sister Card.' Learn it, live it, love it and call it yours because God and everyone takes it. The KSC isn't like Diner's Club, bucko. Think of it as an American Express Centurion card."

The wolf narrowed his eyes, but what could he say? Two days ago, Scarlet mated the Ruling Alpha Pair of North America. Basically, she was now the Queen Beyotch. And having way too much fun with her new position.

The organizer closed his eyes and took a deep breath, releasing it slowly. His fur receded and disappeared into his skin. That done, he returned his attention to Scarlet.

"Apologies, Alpha Mate." The words were shoved through gritted teeth, and sounded less than sincere, but her sister didn't seem to care.

Nope, it looked like Scarlet just wanted to poke the werewolf a little more. She patted him on the head. "It's okay, little puppy." Not waiting for a response from the wolf, Scarlet turned to Whitney and looped their arms together. "Come on, you can tell me why you're all homicidal and suicidal. 'Cause even if you try to kill Callum, he'll end up eating you in a bad way. Then Madden would have to kill him, and it'd all be a big mess. I don't do cleaning."

Whit dug in her heels and shot a glare over her shoulder at the still fuming Callum. "*Someone*, informed me the Ruling Wardens are discussing *legitimate* wolf concerns this morning. Can you believe that? Legitimate!"

Scarlet patted her hand, much like she'd done to Callum's head moments before. "It's okay. They'll learn that you're the most legitimate concern they've ever met. I'll have one of the guys bite 'em."

Her sister glanced around the hallway, and Whitney echoed the move. They were surrounded by werewolves. Some were singles—wolves hoping to meet their werewolf mate at the Gathering. That was another thing that sucked. Alpha Pairs only got to mate with Marked women while individual wolves only mated with other wolves.

Single, unmarked humans got zip.

With a resigned sigh, Scarlet tugged her farther along the hall. "Come on, there's too many super-powered ears here. Let's go somewhere else and rehash the whole you oveinglay the ardensway thingy."

Several snorts echoed around them, and heat suffused Whitney's face. "Seriously? Did you think no one would know pig Latin? Really?"

Besides, she didn't want to have a redo of the conversation she'd had with her sisters at breakfast…

"So, Whitney, why were you eye fucking Emmett and Levy? You know the two non-hot, non-sexy Wardens?" Gabby did the whole smirking thing. Bitch.

Whitney refused to look at her, flicking a crumb off her skirt instead. "I have no idea what you're talking about."

"Liar." Scarlet and Gabby said in unison.

Whit sighed and turned to them. "What did it feel like when you realized that you'd found your mates? I mean, besides the Mark stuff. I'm talking about everything else." She couldn't deny the shaky vulnerability that tinged her voice. "Because… Because maybe… maybe they're mine?"

Then it'd gone on to screeching, general bitching about the Wardens' jerked-off-ed-ness starting with their tardiness and ending with their inability to do anything but regurgitate laws. They also added the idea that maybe Whitney had been dropped on her head as a child. Multiple times. Intentionally maybe, because she'd been rather obnoxious as they grew up. Bitches.

It didn't matter, though. Her conversation with Callum simply reinforced the differences between her and the wolves. There was no respect or tolerance for humans, Alpha Mate's sister or not.

The Ruling Wardens had been dick-esque the previous night when they'd finally shown up. They'd refused to put a stop to Gabby's Challenge. Some stupid whore-wolf wanted Gab's mates. Her sister, of course, told the woman to take a hike and then the wolf-girl had Challenged Gabs for the right to mate Berke and Jack. Not that it was possible for the woman to belong to Berke and Jack, but the psycho chick had it in her head that she was their mate and not Gabriella. The woman was bat-shit crazy. The Challenge consisted of a wolf… against a human. Marked or not, the middle Wickham sister couldn't grow fangs and claws. The Ruling Wardens, Emmett and Levy, spouted the jerk version of "suck it up, buttercup."

Instead of wanting to climb them like Mount Everest and plant her flag, she should have run fast and far. Because it was love-slash-lust at first sight. Well, until Callum reminded her of the whole jerk thing.

Scarlet sighed and tugged on her arm again. "I thought they'd be too dumb to pick up on pig Latin." Growls surrounded them and her sister simply smiled wide and glanced at the people surrounding them. "Look at how much fun it is to make them angry?"

With a giggle, she yanked even harder and Whitney had no choice but to follow her from the area. Death wish. Scarlet had a death wish.

Trailing in her eldest sister's wake, they tromped down the wide hallway. But instead of inching along the wall, Scarlet cut a swath down the center. She giggled more and more with every step as they slipped through the increasing crowd. At some point, Whitney was sure she heard a comment about the "parting of the furry sea."

It was Sunday, the last day of the Gathering. It was also the last few meetings to undergo the Tests of Proximity to see if attending Alpha Pairs could find their mates among the Marked women present. The Ruling Alphas, Madden and Keller, had gotten lucky in finding and mating Scarlet on Friday evening. The Captain of the Guard and his Lieutenant, Berke and Jack, had been equally lucky in snaring

Gabriella on Saturday. The others still hanging around were hoping to have the same sort of good fortune.

They meandered, Whitney shuffling in Scarlet's wake. At least until they were stopped by a huffing and puffing Callum.

"Misses Wickham! Misses—" She and Scarlet turned toward the approaching wolf. "Miss Wickham, Whitney, the Ruling Wardens—" He heaved in a great breath.

"You know, Callum, you really need to add some cardio to your routine. Build up that endurance. I recommend Tae Bo."

Whitney looked to her sister with her eyebrow raised. "Really? You're giving him workout advice? When was the last time you actually did anything other than walk to the elevator?"

Scarlet scoffed. "Duh, you've heard me 'workout' like, all the time since I mated Madden and Keller."

"I don't think letting them worship you sexually counts."

Her sister rolled her eyes. "Of course it does. I get all sweaty."

"With *their* sweat."

"You know what—"

"Misses Wickham, *please*."

That got Whitney's attention. "Look at that, he said please and everything." She smiled. "I don't think I wanna stab you in the eye anymore. Unless you're about to bust out with another 'legitimate.' Then it's on. I will so tap dance all over your furry butt."

Scarlet snorted. "Tap dance?"

"What?" She glared at both of them and settled on her sister. "You have Tae Bo, Gabby has P90X. I tap. There's metal on the bottom of my shoes. They're dangerous." She nodded to emphasize her statement and then pointed at Callum. "You just better be thankful I never took up clogging."

Callum did not look impressed. "Right." He cleared his throat. "I have spoken, with the Ruling Wardens and they have agreed to see you now."

She wanted to have Callum tell Emmett and Levy to go screw themselves. She wanted him to pass along the message that she hoped they took their high-and-mighty butts over the edge of a cliff. She *wanted* to have him convey that she was definitely not attracted-slash-half-in-love-with the two superiority-complex having jerks.

Instead, she smiled, even if Scarlet huffed, and was as polite as possible. "Great. It's about time they took off their ass-hats."

Callum picked up his earlier growling and Scarlet was quick to jump in. "Tut-tut, wolf-boy. She's still holding the Kickass Sister Card."

Callum silenced immediately, his face turning a fun red, and he tilted his head in invitation. "Please, follow me."

"See? There's a benefit to your sister banging the HFICs."

"What?"

"The Head Furballs in Charge." Scarlet gave her a wink and an unrepentant grin. "Now, go kick some ass. I'll check up with you later since, I've got some, uh... Screw it, I need my mates." With that, her sister was gone, weaving her way back the way they'd come.

Finally, Callum opened a heavy door, and the portal swung wide to reveal the Ruling Wardens.

Tentatively, expecting them to pounce at any moment, she edged into the room. Maybe complaining until they agreed to meet with her had been a mistake.

The room was as grand as the rest of the hotel with its plush furnishings, authentic antiques and gold plated fixtures. Heavily cushioned, comfortable chairs surrounded the round, dark wood table and more than one set of claw marks marred the surface.

A sliver of desire shoved at her annoyance as she met Emmett's brown-eyed gaze. Well, her attention remained on his eyes for all of half a second. It wandered farther to the line of his jaw and scruff that decorated his cheeks, then on to his broad shoulders and heavily muscled chest. She was about to keep on going and get to the good stuff when her focus was snared by Levy. He leaned forward and placed his palms on the table that separated them.

"Miss Wickham?"

Was she drooling? Whitney wiped the corner of her mouth and stared at Levy who glared at her in all of his blond hair, blue-eyed glory. A hint shorter than his fellow Warden, he was no less gorgeous or coated in muscles.

Scarlet had definitely been right on two counts: 1) werewolves had never seen an "ugly stick" and 2) they probably should have had the "Whitney being in ovelay with the ardensway" conversation.

*

It hadn't been a fluke, a trick of lighting, or even a tiny mistake. Nope, Levy still desired Whitney Wickham. *Craved.*

He'd caught her scent the previous night while he'd dealt with Gabby's Challenge. The delicate flavors called to his wolf, but he'd brushed them aside. He'd had larger issues at the time. Even this morning, he and Emmett endured meeting after meeting with various wolves. Long standing disputes were brought to them during every Gathering, and this year was no different. Being the Ruling Wardens came with as many drawbacks as perks.

A perk was the magic.

A drawback was the fact no matter how badly he and his wolf desired Whitney, he could never have her. He glanced at his partner and friend; *they* could never have her.

"Miss Wickham, please have a seat." Emmett picked up where Levy left off, gesturing to one of the chairs opposite them.

His partner's hand trembled and he sensed Emmett's attraction to Whitney through their connection. Just as Alpha Pairs were mentally tied to each other, so were Warden Pairs.

Emmett? Levy spoke to his partner telepathically. He was normally the one that had difficulty controlling himself. His magic was always looking for a moment to break free of him, but it seemed Whitney's presence was pushing the other wolf to the edge.

Fuck, Levy… Emmett took a deep breath. Have you ever smelled anything so delicious?

No, he hadn't. He'd never seen anything so appetizing, either.

Her shining brown hair was long, ends curling in rolling ringlets that draped over her shoulders while other lengths rested atop her lush breasts. The strands were like chocolate icing, begging him to come and taste her. It wasn't just her breasts that were full, though. No, her whole body was layered in curves, ones he ached to trace with his tongue. In the human world, she'd be considered overweight. In theirs, she was perfect. Every inch of her made for him, for them.

Then again, she wasn't. The laws were strict and older than anyone knew. It was illegal for a Warden to form a lasting attachment to a female. The risk of the woman influencing the Wardens was too great. The belief was the Warden magic, the bit of something extra inside them, didn't leave room for the mating of souls. Too many Pairs had committed to a female and then all hell had broken loose. There hadn't been a mating since it became known that Wardens didn't have fated mates, even though the emotional connection existed. Laws had been created to make it flat out illegal to even try.

Whitney slipped into the chair, fingers clutched before her and pressed against the tabletop. Her thick thighs connected to wide hips that would cradle him while he…

Levy cleared his throat and willed his cock to soften. He'd been half-erect since she walked through the door, but the idea of sinking into her wetness had him hardening fully and throbbing in his slacks.

"We understand you have an issue you have deemed important enough to bring to our attention." When the first hint of red rushed to her face, he winced and realized he sounded like an ass. The two of them had done the same thing the previous night.

Whitney pressed her lips together until they became a thin, white line slashing across her flushed face. "Yes, I have a *legitimate*," she glared at Callum standing nearby and Levy held back his growl. The lower-ranked wolf had obviously done something to upset her. "A *very legitimate*, concern."

Emmett leaned forward and took a deep, audible breath, coaxing Levy to do the same. Oh, shit, he shouldn't have. The first hint of her scent struck him like a brick to the face. Whitney's flavors reminded him of the rushing river near where they grew up, combined with the alluring scent of honeysuckle. He wanted to lap at her skin and see if she truly did taste like that sweet flower's nectar.

"Explain." Emmett barked the word, the man's gaze focused entirely on a very pissed Callum, and a stinging whip of energy crossed the room. Whitney flinched at his friend's tone, but it was Callum who whimpered and scurried from their presence.

Levy glared at Emmett and then reached across the table. He gave in to the wolf's desire to touch the woman. Just once. He wasn't breaking any laws by simply touching her. A touch wasn't a human marriage. The wolf nudged and prodded him, encouraging him to feel the silkiness of her skin and commit it to memory.

He rested his palm on her fisted hands and squeezed, biting back his smile when a shiver raced through her. Releasing her, he leaned back into his chair and kept his tone neutral. "Miss Wickham, please explain."

13

"As you know, I was 'invited,'" adorably, she used air quotes, "to this year's Gathering along with Scarlet and Gabriella."

He and Emmett nodded in acknowledgement and he stole a closer look at his partner. A quick inventory revealed the man was in a state similar to his own. His nails were darkened due to his beast pushing through. A light dusting of white fur on his arms and his eyes were already taking on the lightened hue of his magic nudging forward.

Levy had to make sure the man's irises didn't go pure white. Hell, he needed to worry about his own, as well. The first rule they'd learned together years ago was to never allow the magic to gain control. The wolf was a beast with an animal's black and white understanding of the world, but it was predictable. The magic that lingered in their blood… was not. It weighed and measured and made decisions that pleased it and not others. Wolves understood dominance and submitting to more powerful beasts. Magic was more like a three-year-old with immeasurable power. It wanted what it wanted and damn everyone else. Even if "everyone else" was the planet's population.

"Unfortunately, I was 'invited' to the Gathering," air quotes again. He wondered if she'd be using them throughout their conversation. He hoped not since it played havoc on his control. Even in her anger, she was beautiful and he wanted to kiss away her sarcastic frown. "And the Gathering is meant for Alpha Pairs to find their mate. A mate that has a Mark." She had a tempting mole along the top curve of her left breast. He wanted to trace it with his tongue. "Thing about it is, I don't have one."

That brought him up short. "What?"

Emmett growled and Levy reached over and squeezed his partner's shoulder. The same feelings coursing through him also flooded Emmett: confusion at how she'd come to be at the Gathering warred with rage at the idea of her actually being Marked and potentially mating with an Alpha Pair.

"I. Don't. Have. A. Mark." She tilted her head to the side, so like a wolf examining something. "Did the class not understand? I don't know sign language, but I'm pretty sure they have a Rosetta Stone program for it."

"Miss Wickham…"

"For the love of—" she huffed. "My name is Whitney and you mean to tell me you have *no* clue about why I'm sitting here? I thought that whole 'tell me why you're here' thing was some throw back to a therapy session gone wrong. Did you seriously not bother listening to any of the messages Keller and Madden left for you about me?" Shit, her face was near glowing red now, and tears glistened in her eyes.

He cursed himself for both his ham-handed handling of her as well as getting caught up in his position. He knew her upset was their fault. He vaguely remembered Keller talking about his new mate-in-law and there being some problem… But then…

Whitney's chest rose and fell in rapid succession, her heavy breathing now audible in the small room.

"Whitney—"

"Oh, bite me."

"Gladly." Emmett leapt to his feet and rounded the table in the blink of an eye, his magic and wolf lending a hand. His voice was rough and deep. Damn, his eyes were whiter than brown or even amber.

15

When his partner reached for her hand, she snatched it back and leaned deeper into the seat. Her anger permeated the air, the scent spicy and hot, arousing him further as it mingled with the delicate honeysuckle that clung to her skin. His fangs elongated, pricking his gums and then lowering until the tips rested against his lower lip. The wolf surged forward, lured by her burgeoning rage.

It wanted to bite her, wanted to take her up on her dare and sink his teeth into her flesh. His eyes zeroed in on his desired spot, where her neck and shoulder met. Right where… Where he was never, ever allowed to go.

Fucking laws.

Fucking magic.

"Let's sit down and discuss this calmly." Levy had to get the meeting back under control because Emmett sure as hell wasn't handling things. His friend glared at him and took another step toward Whitney. "Emmett. Sit down."

He was having enough trouble controlling his own fucking wolf, he didn't need Emmett slipping his leash, too. Growling, his friend finally retreated and slumped into the chair beside him. As soon as it appeared the wolf was in for the long haul, Levy retook his seat.

"Okay, passions," Whitney blushed and his words, taunting Levy once again, "are obviously running high. We apologize for not discussing this previously. Please tell us what happened."

Whitney rubbed her head and her headache was like a physical thing inside him, pulsing within his mind. He shot a questioning glance to Emmett followed by a mental prodding. *Em?*

Yeah, I got it, too. The voice echoed and he mentally groaned. *I shouldn't, but I do.*

Empathy and telekinesis weren't something the two of them had ever shared beyond themselves.

"On the morning of our thirtieth birthday—"

Emmett cut in. "You, Scarlet and Gabriella?" She glared at Emmett and Levy decided he wouldn't be the one to interrupt her next.

"Yes. We're fraternal triplets. Each of us received an 'invitation,'" air quotes again. It seemed she *would* be using them when describing the summons. "At the exact moment of our births, in order. Unfortunately, they'd forgotten about the whole hitting thirty unmated rule and freaked." Whitney snorted. "Scarlet actually tried to burn hers."

Levy furrowed his brow. "Why would she do that? Being mated is an hono—"

She held up a hand. "If you're about to say 'honor,' stuff it. Getting sniffed, patted on the ass, bitten, and then hauled to God knows where without a say in the matter isn't an honor. It's why both of them were so freaked. They're happy. Now. But I know the two of them have dreaded finding their mates. A Marked's life gets uprooted because some mutt sniffs her ass and—"

"No one sniffs you," Emmett growled. Again.

"Of course not." She released a shuddering breath and he ached to go to her. Something about this caused her anger and pain. He didn't want her to ever experience either.

17

"Thank you for your interpretation of the process. That's obviously something that can be discussed at a later time." Any other time when Levy's wolf wasn't about to tear him in two. "Let's get back on track." Before he threw her on top of the table and claimed her and sentenced them to a life worse than death—a life locked in wolf form, never to be released again.

"Fine. We got 'invitations.' They're Marked, I'm not. I'm human, but I got my butt hauled here. Then, you two took your merry time getting here. You didn't even bother to, I don't know, open a book to see if you screwed up your mojo or something."

Regardless of his desire for Whitney, Levy's wolf bristled at the implication they'd failed at their jobs. "We are the Ruling Wardens of North America, the most powerful and skilled Wardens ever born. There was absolutely nothing wrong with the spell we—"

"So, if it's not you, it's me?" Her eyebrows nearly met her hairline.

This time it was rage that poured off her. It blanketed the room and consumed his mind. The wolf and his magic rebelled at the idea she was mad at them and he opened his mouth to soothe her.

Whitney rose to her feet and planted her fists on her hips, accentuating the dip and flare of her waist. She needed to stop tempting him. "Really? That's what you're gonna go with?" She pointed at him, then Emmett. "You two need to figure out what the heck went wrong. You've had since Friday evening and it's now Sunday. How hard is it to hop onto the World Wide Werewolf Web and find an answer?"

Grumbling, she spun and headed toward the door.

No. She couldn't leave. Levy's wolf growled and snarled, the animal manifesting itself beneath his skin, physically scraping against the thin membrane. Darkened nails slid along his arms from inside him. He shuddered with the effort of holding it at bay. The tremors increased when his power shoved at him as well. The magic crackled over him, pricking and biting into him with the desire to be released. It'd detain her, wrap her in a cocoon and then strip her bare for them.

"Whitney, wait." He took a step toward her, then another, rounding the table and closing the distance between them.

Whitney Wickham, woman who drew him in like no other, turned to him. "You know what, fuck you. Fuck you both."

CHAPTER TWO

Whitney shook—with anger or need?—from head to toe. Emotions battered her from all angles. Inside she was a jumble of confusion and desire. It felt as if her body was being pounded by rage, frustration, and all-consuming desperation for release coming from the air.

The anger fueled hers, the frustration at desiring the two wolves fanned the flames, and their seeming carelessness with her problem just sealed their coffin. She'd worked through this already, darn it. It'd taken her years of fighting her inner-self, but she'd finally gotten over craving two wolves as mates. Then she'd met Emmett and Levy and the desires reared their ugly heads once again.

Damn it, damn it, damn it.

She reached for the door's handle, intent on getting the heck away from them as soon as possible. There was a year before the next Gathering. They could figure it out within the coming 365 days without her.

The door groaned as it opened and she tugged harder against the solid panel, only to have her ticket out of the room slammed closed. A heavy weight settled against her back. The heated breath of one of the men bathed her neck for barely a moment and then she was whirled around. She was pressed against the once open door, Emmett crowding her, his warmth and heavenly scent surrounding her.

"Fuck you? Don't mind if I do." A smirk graced his lips.

She should tell him to screw off, to get away from her, to stop touching and arousing her and making her crave him like a drug. She should. But the need in his gaze froze the words in her throat.

Then Levy was there, snug against her right, nudging Emmett to her left. She was bracketed by the large, very aroused Ruling Wardens. Their hard cocks branded her hips and she shuddered. She was pissed and aroused in equal measure. Being more aroused than pissed, pissed her off even more.

Both men inhaled deeply—their chests expanding with the action to brush against her breasts—and growled in unison. Great. They scented her juices. Stupid wolves.

Whitney squirmed, attempted to push her way past the overwhelming males, but they stopped her with partially shifted hands. Levy's arm snaked over her lower stomach, hand coming to rest on her hip. Emmett slid his palm up her ribcage and halted beneath her left breast. The heat of their touch warmed her from inside out, teasing and tormenting in equal measure.

No. She was pissed at them. Pissed because she wanted them and couldn't have them. Pissed that they had been jerks. Pissed that they hadn't bothered researching…

Oh. Wait a minute.

Emmett nuzzled her, his rough cheek scraping the tender skin of her neck and she couldn't suppress her moan. Her sound was answered by Levy as he mimicked his fellow Warden. Two mouths danced over her exposed flesh, tongues lapping at her and teeth scratching her throat. Her pussy clenched, growing heavier and aching more as each second passed.

They kneaded the flesh they held, hands wandering and stroking her. Emmett eased his touch higher, skimming her breast and finally cupping the heavy weight. Levy slid to her center, rubbing her lower belly before going even... lower. His fingers came to rest above her mound, the heat and pressure adding to her need.

Damn her clothing.

Oh. Wait another minute.

Emmett tormented her breast, fingers plucking her nipple and pinching the hardened nub while Levy traveled farther south. His hand skimmed the silken fabric of her skirt and, bending down, he snared the hem before disappearing beneath the flimsy covering. His callused palm scraped her skin, leaving goose bumps in his wake. The higher he rose, the needier she became, her pussy dampening more and more.

As wrong as it was for her, she wanted them both.

Levy neared her heat and she spread her legs farther, granting him unspoken access to where she desired him— *them*—most. He growled when his palm met the juncture of her thighs and she whimpered with the first wave of pleasure his firm touch drew forth.

Whitney burned for them, body desperate for their possession. Unbidden, she slid her palms along their abdomens and on, hunting what she desired. Then she moaned when she found what she sought. The thick ridge of their cocks pulsed beneath her hands, the cloth of their jeans the only thing keeping her from feeling the heat of their dicks. She rubbed and stroked them, sliding up and down their lengths.

Their moans turned into growls and those wicked mouths continued their torment. Nips, licks, scrapes, and nibbles rained down on her shoulders and throat. Pleasure assaulted her, raced through her from head to toe and she couldn't withhold the groans and gasps that built inside her.

She shuddered and writhed, kicking at her conscience every time it piped up in protest. She wanted this even if it was wrong. She could have regrets… later. Much, much later. For now she would live out her lifelong fantasies.

Emmett's touch floated away and she whined at the loss only to moan when he returned… under her top, inside her bra, bare hand now cupping and caressing her breast.

"Yes," she hissed and then Levy's fingers slipped beneath the elastic of her panties to stroke her soaked flesh. "Oh, fuck, yes."

It wouldn't take much, no more than a few flicks of her clit, and she'd come screaming their names.

Levy slipped a single digit between her sex lips, the rough pad of his finger sliding over that bundle of nerves and she rocked her hips into the caress. All the while, she stroked them and hoped she gave them the same pleasure they gifted her.

"Please…" She whimpered and they growled, one immediately following the other.

Emmett's touch became more firm, plucking and flicking her nipple until she thought she'd go crazy with the need for them. Once again he retreated, but then cool air bathed her breast before a heated, wet mouth captured her nipple. He tapped the hardened nub with his tongue, licking and suckling that bit of flesh. Every pull sent another bolt of pleasure through her body, drawing her closer and closer to release.

Their touch, their scent, their very presence hurtled her toward the edge. Pleasure coursed through her veins in ever increasing speed, pricking her nerve endings and sending shudders through her body.

Seeming to sense her impending orgasm, their attentions increased. Touches grew more firm, kisses and nibbles became more passionate, and Levy's teasing caresses focused on her clit.

"God. Yes. Need." Whitney needed *so* bad.

A low, grumbled "mine" from Levy was immediately echoed by Emmett and she promised herself she'd bitch at them about tossing that word around later. Like, after she came. Wolves couldn't toy with a woman that way. She, hypothetically, accepted this would be a onetime thing. It was her single chance to get her ovelay for the ardensway out of her system for good.

Whitney squeezed and stroked the cocks pulsing beneath her palms, milking them in the same rhythm that they tormented her. She rocked and writhed against Levy's hand, begging and directing his ministrations in equal measure.

Just a little more…

"There. So close, please please please please." Her words came out as heavy, panting moans and whines.

Twin stings jolted her, a hint of pain searing her nipple and shoulder at the same moment and she went flying over the edge. Her release washed through her in a gigantic wave. Her nerve endings flared to life, seeming to burn her from inside out as the bliss flooded her. Whitney's pussy clenched, silently begging to be filled and stretched by their thick cocks. She wanted them hard and deep, plunging into her over and over again.

Another bolt of hurt slid through her and then she burned. Her skin was on fire, scorching under the heat of their touch. Sensations bombarded her, emotions rioting and pinging around her body. Emotions—hers or theirs?—slammed into her, one upon on another upon another.

Want.

Need.

Possessiveness.

Domination.

Love.

The love bit definitely belonged to her. But some of the other feelings…

Agony possessed her and she gasped, the ache snatching away the lingering pleasure of her release. She jerked and twisted, fighting against the throbbing that plagued her.

Whitney's skin stretched and tightened, as if the air sucked every hint of moisture from her. With the next wave of agonizing pain, she wrenched from their grasp and fell to her knees. Her heart thundered and her lungs heaved with the effort of simply pulling air into her body.

It hit her again, twining around every nerve ending and squeezing until her vision greyed. The pain intensified, the feeling of a thousand snakes pricking and gouging her skin overwhelming her while the light in the room faded further.

The greatest orgasm of her life and it was gonna kill her. As soon as she was done dying, she was so gonna open a can of Wickham whoop-ass on those wolves.

*

Emmett's heart stopped when Whitney's knees hit the ground and it shattered when she crumpled to the plush carpet. He flew to her side, wolf and magic granting him the ability to catch her before more than her hands touched the ground.

The arousal and feral need for her had been replaced by fear the moment her first cry of pain hit the air. That sound was immediately followed by unseen fists pummeling him with her agony.

He gripped her arms, turning her and then cradling her to his chest. Her body was hot, scorching and burning him with the heat. Her skin bubbled and stretched, inflating and then sinking back into place with an ever-increasing pace. She whimpered and moaned, twitching and jerking against his hold but he held her still.

"Levy?" He didn't hold back the fear in his voice.

"Fuck. I don't know, man." His partner's hands hovered just above her, the same worry tinging his words.

The temperature of her skin grew, increasing with every rapid beat of her heart. The tempo of her breathing doubled. Moments ago, he would have taken pleasure in the way her breasts bounced with each inhale. Now he dreaded what was to come.

Emmett's wolf alternated between triumph and worry, howling and growling in equal measure. It urged him toward joy at her… transition? The magic—the *other*—pushed the same emotion forward. Possessiveness filled him. She was his. Theirs. No one could part them after the afternoon's events. The wolf and the *other* were confident in that fact.

Whitney arched and struggled against his hold, but he didn't relent. Not when her tiny, human nails dug into his flesh. Or when his skin burned so hot it charred.

"What the fuck?" Levy jumped to assist him; his friend's hands gripping Whitney's legs and ceasing her struggles. "We need help, man."

No. No, they didn't. Emmett shook his head. "No. It's… It's almost over."

Whatever "it" was. The *other* part of him, his magic, was sure the end was near.

Emotions battered him. His. Levy's. Whitney's?

No, sensing other's feelings wasn't one of his gifts. Yet hadn't he felt her earlier?

Her agony plowed into him with every hummingbird-fast beat of her heart and anger assaulted him each time her muscles twitched. Attraction, desire, affection akin to love, poured forward in tsunami-like waves. They had to come from her, especially that last emotion. He'd never allow his heart to venture there. Not with the laws governing Wardens. Never.

The air surrounding them crackled, drying and sharpening as if he and Levy called on their magic. But they weren't. Who was?

"Levy?" He couldn't afford to split his attention between the person gathering all their power and Whitney.

"On it." His friend's hands remained in place, and Levy closed his eyes, casting his powerful net and hunting for the stranger draining them.

Whitney jerked and cried out, back bowed. Her mouth stretched wide, and the breath in her lungs stilled, a scream bursting from her lips.

"Oh fuck." Levy's voice was barely audible.

Her muscles tightened and stretched farther.

"Oh fuck. It's her." Awe and fear filled his partner's words. "It's Whitney."

"Wha—" Emmett didn't get a chance to finish his question or process the fact a human woman was syphoning their power.

A pulse of magic larger and stronger than anything he'd ever experienced pushed from the beautiful woman in his arms. It flowed through her; it *was* her. The skin that'd burned and bubbled like molten fire now smoothed and glowed like the full moon. It throbbed with power similar to his and Levy's yet so very, very different.

It gathered within her, and his body recognized the increasing mass. Beneath his gaze, it slithered under her skin, pressing against the now-translucent barrier. In its wake, symbols formed, twining twirls decorated her arms, shoulders, and chest then on to her legs. He had no doubt they appeared below her clothing, as well.

"What the fuck did we do?" Emmett barely passed the words between his lips.

A glass-shattering scream rent the air, destroying the strained quiet of moments before. Immediately on the heels of the echoing strains of her roar, the room filled with a blinding white light. His vision was clouded by the glow, searing in its intensity, and he blinked past the tears filling his eyes.

The white filled him, sinking into him and wrapping around his heart. It held his very life in its grip, tightening until the steady thump trembled and became uneven. He felt it studying him, judging him—digging through his body and mind—then it released him as quickly as it'd taken him captive. He coughed and gasped, waiting for his organs to steady once again. He risked opening his eyes. The moment he processed the vision before him, he gasped.

Whitney—their Whitney—lay still on the ground as he'd expected but she... glowed. Literally glowed as if the fire and power of the magic she'd torn from them had embed itself in every cell of her body. The twining symbols now burned, light playing along each line and shining in hues that shifted from pink to blue to purple and on and on...

Her body, brightened by the presence of this *other*—magic that filled her from head to foot—and the meaning of the markings became clear.

Whitney didn't have a single Mark like her sisters, proclaiming her potential mating to an Alpha Pair.

She had *hundreds*.

So, what did that mean?

CHAPTER THREE

Whitney woke to harsh whispers, the low sounds bouncing around her mind in a transparent hurricane of altos and tenors. After each snippet, she identified the speaker.

"… you did this…" *Scarlet.*

"… dying?" Gabriella.

"I've never seen…" *Keller.*

"… heard about…" *Madden.*

"… Warden Born…" *Who's that?*

Some voices she recognized, Scarlet's accusatory tone unmistakable as it twined with Gabby's worried voice. That alone was enough to shove her closer to action. She tensed and flexed her muscles, surprised that no pain lingered. She didn't remember much from before she passed out, but she definitely recalled insane pleasure followed by bone-breaking agony.

Thank God the agony had gone on vacation.

Whitney fought the heavy weight holding her lids closed and forced them to open.

Totally a mistake.

The minute her eyes were revealed, pain assaulted her, barraging her with the feeling as if needles attacked the aching orbs. She immediately slammed them shut and a groan reverberated in her chest. A groan that caught the attention of those around her.

"Whitney?" Scarlet's voice pounded against her and another groan was torn from her.

"Shh… Whisper." Whitney shoved the words past her dry throat.

"We are whispering," Gabby's voice boomed.

Fingers stroked her and she jerked from the touch, the pain of the caress sending another shot of agony through her body. She trembled and sunk into the soft surface beneath her, anxious to be away from what caused so much pain. She whimpered and shifted again. She couldn't figure out what was worse: the whispers or the touches.

"Open your eyes, love." The deep tenor drifted to her like a gentle breeze, the familiar voice coaxing her to do as he asked. Emmett's words were so gentle compared to the growling and snarling from… before. How long ago was "before?"

"Bright," she grumbled.

"Turn out the lights." Levy issued the order and she assumed it'd been carried out. "Try now."

Preparing herself for the inevitable pain, she sighed in resignation and did as he bid. When a man like Levy spoke so softly and sweetly, she couldn't help but listen. Carefully, and oh so slowly, she lifted her eyelids once again. She raised them in tiny increments, bringing the world into focus a sliver at a time.

"Lights are still on," she whimpered.

"Um…" Emmett's voice trailed off. "Just try for us, love."

She sighed and did as he asked. Before long, the room materialized before her and that low glow still pervaded the space. "Did it. Close. Bright."

Didn't they understand that? Were they freakin' blind?

Levy came into focus, his face and body filling her vision, and the man looked worried and nervous as hell. "Sweet, I'm going to hold your hand, okay? Just let me show you… something."

His rough, callused fingers slid over her skin and she braced for the pain surely to come as it had when her sister's had touched her. Only… it didn't. Maybe that was done and gone. At least, she hoped.

As promised, her hand replaced the wolf in her line of sight.

Her glowing hand.

Her glowing, with weird lines all over it, hand.

Wait, back it up. Glowing. And the lines weren't stripes or squiggles, but had a definite shape and pattern. They pulsed with an iridescent light, the rainbow of colors flowing along each curve. And they looked like, exactly like, her sister's Marks.

But all over.

"What. The. Fuck?" The words were raspy, but she got them out.

"We, uh, don't know." Emmett's words were timid and that snared her attention. He was a Ruling Warden, one half of the most powerful Warden Pair in North America. The werewolf didn't have a timid bone in his body.

"We have a guess." Hell, even Levy wasn't sure of himself.

"And what, pray tell, is our guess," she licked her lips and swallowed, her panic quickly overcoming any pain that lingered. "As to why I suddenly resemble a graffiti covered glow stick?"

Scarlet popped into her vision, and this time, she really did whisper. "We were thinking more like a freakily tattooed firefly. But you haven't blinked yet. Could you blink?" The innocence in her gaze lasted less than a second and then a wicked grin graced her features.

"Nah, not a lightning bug. I vote for night light." Gabby nudged Emmett aside. "I mean, you won't ever need one again."

It was just like her sisters to use jokes to cover the scary drama. Like that one time Gabby had broken her leg when trying to prove she could fly and they'd joked and laughed the whole way home. Well, Scarlet joked and Whitney laughed. Gabby spent a lot of time sniffling and cursing them. They'd been ten.

Whitney raised her hand once again, staring at her fingers, palm and then arm in awe. Somehow, someway, her bow-chicka-bow-bow-ish-ness resulted in a Day Glo body.

"Emmett?" Even if he'd been the growlier and jerkier of the two Wardens, she reached for him first. Beyond the man's asshole-esque behavior lurked a protective need that exceeded even Scarlet's mate Madden. "Levy?" Although she called him second, she knew he'd temper Emmett and provide an easy soothing she needed.

Scarlet and Gabby were nudged aside and then the men were there, bracketing her as they had moments ago. Moments? "How long was I out?"

Levy grimaced. "Six hours."

"Scared the hell out of us." Emmett glared. "Don't do it again."

A grin eased to her lips. "I'll try. We really don't know what this is?"

Her blond wolf looked away, his attention fixed across the room as he spoke. "We have a guess." He slipped his hand beneath her neck, and Emmett was quick to mirror his movements. "Let's sit you up and then we can tell you what we know."

"What we *think* we know," Scarlet interjected. "You two and Gandalf here don't have a clear answer."

Twin growls surrounded her and despite her pain, she was quick to pet and soothe them. "Let's just talk."

Both men nodded and amidst her grunts and groans they got her vertical-ish. It was then she realized she sat in the middle of a massive king sized bed inside a gigantic bedroom. Clothes were scattered over every surface, shirts and shorts fighting for space with the evidence of meals rested on tables, chairs, and dressers. The tempting scents of freshly cut wood, dew-covered grass, and male musk surrounded her.

A man's room. No, *her* men's room. She'd been brought to their den.

Sitting up, she also saw the others surrounding her. Scarlet stood in the circle of her mate's arms, Keller and Madden stroking her sister. Gabriella was in a similar state as she leaned against Berke's chest while Jack pressed against her back.

It was the other male in the area that was unfamiliar. Positioned near the door, an older man—*must be "Gandalf"*—stood stock still, his eyes intent on her. For some reason, she felt compelled to take a deep breath and analyze the scents in the room. *A wolf. Old. Weak.* She didn't ponder how she knew those things about the strange male. Not at all.

"Miss Wickham—"

"Whitney," she was quick to correct him.

His eyes narrowed a moment, but the hint of dislike was gone before she could question him. "Whitney, I think I may know what has happened, but I'll need your version of events."

"Version of events?" She looked to Emmett, then Levy, with her eyebrows raised. The massive males had the grace to blush.

"Yeah, love, all of it."

Now it was *her* turn to blush. "Um, I met with Emmett and Levy—"

"You mean the Ruling Wardens of North America." That distaste was back.

"Yes, but considering Emmett had a good old time under my shirt and Levy had his hand in my panties, I think using their first names is appropriate," she snapped. "Especially since the two of them turned me into a glow stick." Her voice rose with every word as hot anger suffused her. It felt like her earlier ire yet so much more.

"Easy, sweet." Levy stroked her arm and she leaned into the touch, the emotions fleeing as quickly as they'd arrived.

Crap, going Day Glo had really messed with her head.

Gandalf glared for a moment, but the instant all eyes returned to him, the look vanished and a concerned expression graced his features.

Oh, she didn't trust this guy. He had something against her, the situation, and she was waiting for him to snap.

"Very well. Continue." All that was missing was the condescending flip of his hand.

"First, what the hell is your name? Why should I tell you anything?" Bitch, party of one.

Emmett cleared his throat. "This is Elder Warden Sarvis. He was our mentor while we trained as Wardens as well as our surrogate father since training requires children to be taken away from their parents at a young age."

Damn, apparently she'd have to be nice to the guy. "I see." She pasted a bright smile on her face, internally wincing at the sting. "I'm so sorry." *Liar.* "This whole thing has my head a little turned around."

"Accepted. Continue." The jerk did do the whole hand flippy thing that time.

Something inside her burned and bristled at his tone and attitude, but she didn't have time to examine the strange feelings coursing through her. She wasn't normally so quick to anger, but now…

"I went to speak to Emmett and Levy about why I was summoned to the Gathering."

"You don't have a Mark."

If the man didn't let her finish her freaking story… "No, prior to being lit up like a lighthouse, I didn't. But I got an 'invitation.'"

He harrumphed. "Impossible. The spell was rewritten—"

She ignored him, and his little 'rewritten' comment, and continued. "They weren't able to tell me anything so I tried to leave. We had words and then we, uh, got intimately acquainted."

Emmett chuckled. "You said 'fuck you' and I accepted *your* invitation."

A heated blush stole over her cheeks and she glared at the wolf.

"Detail your *intimate* encounter."

Whitney narrowed her eyes and then turned her attention to her sisters, specifically Scarlet. The woman was mated to the Ruling Alphas, dang it. Couldn't she stop all this?

Scarlet rolled her eyes. "Just tell him. I mean, you've been listening to us boink all hours of the day. This isn't any more embarrassing than that."

"Fine," she huffed. "Emmett and my breast had a wonderful meeting of the mouths while Levy shook hands with my pussy. Good enough?" The Elder's face flushed and his anger whipped at her. "Then there was a little sting, a great big orgasm and *boom*, I'm a firework. Are we all happy with rehashing Whitney's embarrassment?"

Through it all the Elder stared at her, his dark gaze seeming to bore into her soul. His eyes flashed amber once or twice, but otherwise, he showed no emotion. "You felt pain at the time of your *completion*?" He said it like a dirty word and she wanted to scratch his eyes out.

"Yes."

Sarvis's attention left her and turned to Emmett and Levy. "You stupid, stupid fools."

Whitney snarled and yanked herself from the wolves' grasp, clawing her way across the bed, intent on swiping the man with her... She glanced down. Holy shit, with her claws. Well, they were claw-ish. More like human hands with suddenly long fingernails.

The Elder gestured toward her, his waving arm encompassing her body. "You see what you've done by violating the laws? What you've created? You've tied this *human* to you and are turning her into an abomination. You began the mating process and this is what's left." He spat the words, flinging the hate filled message at her across the room's expanse.

"Wardens can't mate." Emmett voiced Whitney's first thought.

Instead of answering, the old man pointed at her men. "You started it. You finish it. Permanently. Because this *cannot* continue further."

Dual growls surrounded her, sounds soon followed by those from her sister's mates. Then another joined the echoing threat… hers. Whitney dug her fingers into Emmett and Levy's thighs while the gentle glow that coated her body flared to life. Whatever it was that now lived inside her pulsed and pounded, screamed to be set free and Whitney was bloodthirsty enough to let it.

Growing brighter by the second, Whitney gave the Elder a simple warning.

"You, should be running."

*

Whitney made his cock harder than granite. Emmett's body instantly responded to her threat, dick filling and lengthening with the idea of her tearing someone apart. Hints of shame hit him and overshadowed his arousal, but then she growled and he shoved it aside. He stared at her, noting the flush of her cheeks, the rapid rise and fall of her chest, and the way she licked her lips. She was gorgeous, delicious, and *theirs*.

And regardless of his respect and love for Sarvis, she would remain alive and by their sides. Rage at the older wolf's veiled order and threat swept through him and he remembered the man still lingered in the room.

Emmett's beast, primed and ready for a fight, was anxious to slough off the adrenaline remaining after Whitney's scare. He turned toward his mentor. "She's right. You *should* be running. And pray we don't find you."

Sarvis bared his teeth. "You don't understand. She'll weaken you. Destroy you. The Elders won't stand by while you ruin everything. Women disrupt the balance of power, that's why Warden matings were outlawed. We worked too hard to prevent this and now—" With an echoing snarl, the Elder whirled and flew from the room, the heavy wood door slamming in his wake.

"That guy is a crazy assed douche of epic proportions."

Emmett had learned Gabby wasn't one to mince words.

"Word to our mother." And Scarlet was, occasionally, a woman of few words. Though he didn't always understand them all. She must have noticed the confusion filling the room. "You know, like 'word to your mother,' but we're sisters so it's 'word to our mother?'" She raised her eyebrows. "No? No one is getting this?"

Beside him, Whitney vibrated with barely leashed tension, tremors, and shakes overtaking her at an ever increasing rate and Emmett brushed Scarlet's rambling aside. "Whitney?"

"He wants me dead," she whispered, but Emmett heard her loud and clear.

As did Levy. The wolf growled. "That's not happening."

"Ever." He'd rip apart anyone, wolf or man, who dared come near their mate with harm in mind.

Emmett opened his mouth to explain that he'd gut whoever came near her with malicious intent, but Gabby stepped forward and he swallowed his words.

The middle Wickham sister raised her hand as if in school. "Let's slow our roll and think about something no one else has brought to the table. Whitney is Emmett and Levy's mate. As in *mate*. Like, the Holy Grail, it's a miracle, she's glowing like those weird algae in the ocean, has mad Marks, and she isn't supposed to exist *mate*." Gabby heaved a breath. "Whew, that was a lot to get out." She shook her head. "Point is," Gabby waved a hand at Whitney, "she wasn't supposed to be here, and she is. She isn't supposed to be anyone's mate, and she is. Which—big picture—means the happy little laws you wolf boys—" growls filled the room, Emmett and Levy's included, and the woman rolled her eyes. "Whatevs. The laws are partly based on mistaken beliefs that Wardens don't get mates. That guy said they *outlawed* matings, not that they didn't *exist*. So, those laws you've been clinging to like your favorite chew-toy are wrong. Makes you wonder what else is all made up. And by who?"

Breath stilled in Emmett's lungs, the mere idea…

"What else 'doesn't exist,' but really does? Like vamps. Are they real? Do they sparkle? Are they hot? Because, lemme tell ya, there isn't a wolf alive that's been hit by the ugly stick." Scarlet fanned her face. "Whew. The hotness that surrounds me is—" Keller slapped a hand over Scarlet's mouth.

"Unless you want to be bare-assed over Madden's lap, now would be a good time to be quiet."

Based on Scarlet's expression, Emmett didn't believe she'd mind.

Beside him, Whitney twitched, another jerk reminiscent of the tremors that had overtaken her body hours before. It was enough to pull his attention back to the woman at his side. He moved to stroke her, soothe her with is touch, but froze when his hand hovered less than an inch about her skin. Would it pull a scream from her as it'd done when her sisters had attempted the same?

Emmett didn't have another moment to question himself. Whitney leaned into him with a whimper while she sought out Levy with her other hand. All connected, the touch sent a wave of happiness and calm through him. It eased his wolf's agitation and the frayed edges of his magic smoothed. He hadn't even known he was so close to losing control, and now he realized Sarvis was lucky to be alive.

Whitney shivered, another whimper, and tugged Levy to her other side. He and his partner shared a look, one that said they'd protect her at all cost, she belonged to them, and their feelings went beyond affection, on to lov—

"How old are the Warden laws? Hell, mating laws? When did they pop into existence?" Her voice was strong despite her obviously weakened state. "Like, Texas outlawed dildos in 1973, you know? It's public knowledge. Can I get a date on the mating laws? Maybe Wardens are able to mate with humans. If there can even be the beginning of a mating process, mates for Wardens had to exist at some point. And what about single wolves?"

"I—"

"But—"

He and Levy spoke at the same time. He sensed his partner's disbelief, shock, and growing anger at the realization the laws they'd been living under were nothing more than lies created by demented wolves.

"Dildos? Outlawed?" Scarlet turned to her mates. "We're never going to Texas. I'd be arrested and I'm too annoying to be put in prison. I'd be shanked in a week."

Whitney snorted. "Who are you kidding, you'd rule them all."

Emmett smiled. Despite her fatigue, Whitney was still cracking jokes at her sister's expense. That meant she'd be okay, they'd be okay. The three of them had to get past their current troubles and then they'd be fine.

"Troubles?" Whitney snorted. "Captain Understatement."

Emmett stilled and looked to Levy. "Did I say that out loud?"

"Say what?"

It was Whitney's turn to stiffen. "You didn't…"

He shook his head.

"Which means I read your…"

He nodded.

"Anyone wanna share with the rest of the class?" Gabby pulled everyone's attention.

"I can hear them." Whitney's tone was shaky.

The middle Wickham rolled her eyes. "Duh. You're mated. Mostly. It comes with the gorgeous, yet annoying and domineering, men beside you." Gabby pointed at Whitney. "And no take backs."

Their mate's heart rate soared, breathing increasing until she was near to hyperventilating.

Shit. "Okay, everyone out."

"But—"

"Our sister—"

Levy solved the problem with a booming, echoing roar. "Out!"

*

Breathing was beyond Whitney. Her brain deserted her and movement so wasn't happening. *Mate?*

"Didn't you hear everything, sweet?" Levy rubbed her back, his gentle touch soothing her and her pulse lowered the tiniest bit.

"Sarvis screamed the words, love. You're ours." Emmett's gruff voice filled her ear as he rubbed his chin over her shoulder.

Their bodies, their scents, surrounded and comforted her more than words could ever express. Right there, right then, she was at peace despite the panic that continued to attack her.

This very second was the culmination of her dreams and fantasies. And okay, she had heard the words everyone had been tossing around, but they finally sank in.

At five years old, she'd known she was different from Scarlet and Gabriella.

They'd been homeschooled while Whitney was sent to the local kindergarten.

They learned to read books filled with werewolf stories while she had to see Dick and Jane run.

They played princess and her sisters were always rescued by two princes…

When they played with dolls, they always had two boys and a girl. Every time Whitney had attempted to play the same game, her mother had plucked the extra toy from her hand. That "wasn't for her."

Their mother was never cruel, but the truth had never been hidden from Whitney. Her sisters were Marked, she was not, and that meant their lives would never be the same. A wall stood between the three of them and it'd never, ever be broken. Whitney needed to get over her dreams and accept reality. Scarlet and Gabriella had always included her in everything non-wolf and never made her feel less due to her lack of a Mark, but that wall always remained.

Now she was the same. She glanced at her arm. Okay, she was same-ish.

Tears burned her eyes, she was like them now. She wasn't on the outside looking in, wasn't the little girl who watched her sisters wander off to do those things only the Marked got to do. She wasn't *different*.

The glow emanating from her body pulsed brighter for a brief moment reminding her she was a little different. But at least she had two mates as she'd always dreamed. Her soul had always known a life with one man hadn't been her future. And now everyone else knew, as well.

Still reeling from the acceptance of Sarvis's words, Whitney replayed them in her mind…

You see what you've done by violating the laws? What you've created? You've tied this human to you and are turning her into an abomination. You began the mating process and this is what's left. You started it. You finish it. Permanently. Because this cannot continue further.

"We began the mating process," she whispered the words, still not believing everything that had happened.

Emmett gave her a slow nod and Levy did the same.

"But we didn't finish it. Do you think," she licked her lips, anxiety rising with every syllable she uttered. She hated her insecurities. Hated them. Her sisters were just as curvy as her and their mates worshipped the ground they walked on. Could Emmett and Levy feel the same? "Do you think the world would end if we did finish it? Because that guy said… I mean, if you want, we could. And not right this second. Because you don't have to. Because—"

Levy placed two fingers over her lips, silencing her before she managed to hyperventilate once again. "I don't think it would end the world. You wouldn't have come to us, mated to us, if we weren't destined to be together. Just as Scarlet and Gabriella found their intended mates, so have we."

She weighed Levy's words, the expressions flitting across his face, and analyzed them. The heat in his gaze was unmistakable. The man's wolf peered behind his human eyes, the amber shining past the pale blue. Then a ripple of white slithered through his irises.

"What the hell?" She leaned toward him. "What was that?"

He grimaced, a pained twist of his lips. "Don't be afraid, sweet. We're Wardens and that comes with the wolf and a little something extra."

Vulnerability surrounded him. As she heard Emmett before, she now sensed Levy's emotions. The big, bad wolf was

47

nervous, scared that despite their half-mating, she'd become disgusted and leave him.

Ah, her sensitive wolf. She recognized Emmett's rough, forceful personality with ease, but Levy would be the one she had to worry about hurting. Ferocious wolf or not, he had a gentle heart.

Aching to put him at ease, show that the bit of "extra" didn't bother her, she held up her hand. "Kinda like being glow in the dark?"

Pain suffused the connection between the three of them. A hint of it came from Levy, but a good dose emanated from Emmett. No longer feeling the aches from before, she easily shifted and faced the larger wolf.

"Hey, I'm not mad."

He shook his head. "You didn't see it. My God, love."

She held back the thrill at being called "love." Several times the word had tumbled from his lips and she prayed it wasn't something he tossed around as easily as he breathed.

"You…" Emmett trembled. "We held you in our arms and then you wouldn't stop screaming. Your body… It just…"

Without hesitation, she reached for him, cupped his cheek and leaned forward to brush a soft kiss across his lips. "I'm fine." She looked at the radiant hand pressed to his skin. "Well, fine-ish." She shrugged and took a deep breath then released it slowly. "I don't understand this. I can't even pretend I do." Whitney shifted and rested against the bed's headboard. "But I *can* accept that a wolf knows its mate. I can accept that the feelings I have for you go so far beyond what I've ever felt for any of my exes combined." Twin growls rumbled and vibrated the air around her and she rolled her eyes. "They're exes for a reason, guys. Anyway, I can stretch my reality to accept all of this. But it doesn't change the fact that the man who practically raised you believes I should be 'resolved' permanently."

Emmett stroked the back of her hand, his blunt fingertip tracing the new swirls that covered her skin. "He *did* practically raise us, and the penalty for a Warden mating is severe. The Elders would force our shift and then lock us in animal form for the rest of our lives." Anger coated his features. "We'd go feral simply because we found happiness. I can't believe this is wrong. The spell wouldn't have called you to the Gathering—we wouldn't have found you—if it wasn't meant to be."

Whitney flipped her hand over and gripped his, immediately doing the same and reaching for Levy. "What? They would—"

Levy shook his head. "It's not gonna happen. We're the most powerful Wardens the world has seen." He gently squeezed her. "There's nothing to worry about. When we're ready, we'll complete our mating and—"

She sat up straighter. "When? Like, now? 'When' is now." She nodded so they knew she was serious.

He grimaced and Emmett's face held a similar expression. "Whitney, you don't understand. If a nick did this…"

She shook her head. "No. I think I'm simply stuck somewhere in the middle of not-mated and mated. Normal matings involve more bodily fluids and sticky stuff. We didn't get past second base. Wrapping things up should make it all better. I think. Maybe?" She grinned at them, imagining the pleasure that was surely to come while also praying she was right. "I vote we get to squishy."

They both shook their heads and Levy dropped the news. "No. We'll go back to the Ruling Alpha's compound and dig into the archives. I want to know exactly what's going to happen to you before we risk you further. Someone has to be hiding something… somewhere." He traced circles on her palm. "I care too much to endanger or lose you, Whitney Wickham. If you…" His eyes glistened and he blinked away what had to have been tears. "If something happened to you, if you got hurt because of us, we would go insane." His gaze bore into her. "Feral is the last thing they'd need to worry about. We've never pushed our magic, never explored how far we could truly go, but if you were injured, no one in the world would be safe. No one."

Okay then.

"So, it'd be best, if we held off on boinking until we know you won't level the world." She jerked her head in a quick nod. "Got it."

She didn't agree with them, but she could at least understand their reservations.

"Good." Levy darted forward and pressed a kiss to her forehead then Emmett did the same. "Let's get some sleep."

She snorted and Emmett chuckled.

Levy faux growled. "Shut it, you two. At least lay down. We've got an early flight tomorrow. We'll head to the Ruling Alpha's compound and get the research going while you and your sisters get settled. The real world beckons."

Something deep in Whitney's bones told her things weren't going to unfold as easily as the two men anticipated. Sarvis was... evil. She sensed it as he spewed his filth, glaring at her whenever he felt he could get away with it. The man knew too much about what was happening between her, Levy, and Emmett. He hadn't assumed, he'd recognized what had transpired.

The real world beckons? More like threatens.

Chapter Four

Sleeping between two men she couldn't touch stank. Sleeping between two men who had large, rock hard cocks digging into her sides sucked donkey balls. Twice. On top of that was the worry over what the coming days would bring. The men were too lax for her tastes, at least, on the surface.

Well, she wasn't gonna be laidback on *any* surface.

Wiggling and squirming, Whitney slipped from the bed, leaving a fluffy girl shaped hole between them. She knew she wouldn't have long. All night they'd kept their hands on her, cuddling her between them. She'd been soothed with low grumbles and gentle strokes each time she jerked awake, memories of the pain she'd endured tormenting her.

Grabbing a discarded T-shirt from the ground, she took a whiff and decided it was clean enough to wear. Oversized and so long it fell to her knees, she figured she was covered enough to make it to Scarlet's suite. First, she'd sneak into Gabby's, grab her sister, and then they'd head up the hidden steps and drag Scarlet outta bed. One, two, three, and done.

Whitney tip-toed to the front door, snaring the key card to her sister's suite on the way. Thank goodness they'd all exchanged keys. At the time, it'd been because they shared clothes. Now it was for a little breaking and entering.

The knob turned silently, disengaging and allowing her to ease the door open. She peeked into the hallway, checking to make sure the coast was clear. Carpet stretched from one end of the hall to the other and there wasn't a wolf or human in sight. *Perfect.*

She held her breath, eased from the room and stepped out, ensuring the door clicked closed as quietly as possible. When no growling roars echoed through the hotel, she released the air in her lungs. Whew.

She bolted down the hallway, anxious to get to Gabs and subsequently Scarlet for some girl talk. In moments she stood before her sister's door. The keycard slid in easily, the little green light above the handle blinking to let her know she could commence with breaking and entering.

The interior looked much like Whitney's room, the entryway leading into a massive living room and two bedrooms branched off from the main space. Following the trail of clothing that led to the room on the left, she soon slipped into the trio's bedroom.

And way too much skin was exposed for her liking.

"Gabby," she whispered. Nothing happened. "Gabs, wake up." The damn woman slept like the dead.

Seeing a couple of socks nearby, she snared and balled them, slipping one inside the other. She hefted the light weight. It was just heavy enough to be thrown and hit her sister. Perfect. At least her time playing softball while her sisters studied wolf-land was good for something.

Taking aim, she tossed it at Gabby, smacking her right in the face.

"Wait, wha—" she snuffled. "No more. Tired."

God, she didn't even want to know why Gabs was exhausted. Probably for the opposite reason Whitney *wasn't* tired. "Gabby. I need you."

Her sister finally raised her head, hair sticking in all directions and squinting eyes met hers. "Huh?"

"Come on," she waved her hand, gesturing for her sister to get outta bed.

Groaning, Gabby dropped her head back to the pillow and whispered into the room. "You so owe me. Breakfast. Lots. Coffee. More."

"Done. Come on."

Like a fluffy ninja, her sister wiggled and twisted her way from between her men, similar to what Whitney had done. Several tense seconds later, a very naked Gabriella was free of her sheet-prison. It wasn't until her sister tumbled from the bed that she got an eyeful and Whitney whirled with a squeak. She loved her big sis, she just didn't want to see all of her.

The shuffle of clothes signaled the woman was getting dressed and then they were ready to go. Nearly silent they crept up the stairs.

"Why are we sneaking away?" The whisper seemed like a scream.

Right, *nearly* silent.

"'Cause I said so."

"That only works when you're older than me."

"Bite me."

"That's Emmett and Levy's job."

"I hate you."

"You love me."

God, normal. Normal felt so good.

By then, they'd reached the top of the stairs to find a glaring Scarlet staring at them.

Whitney smiled wide. "You're awake."

"Under protest. The guys had some stupid meeting thing this morning and wanted a quickie before they left. Apparently baby making is number one on their to-do list." The eldest Wickham shuffled to the large couch and flopped onto the cushioned surface. "I think my vagina is going on strike."

"TMI."

"Tough." Scarlet stuck out her tongue. "Why are you here?"

"To talk," Whitney nibbled her lower lip.

"Come on then. Order me some breakfast and pull up a seat."

A nearby guard stepped forward and Whitney didn't even flinch. Crazy how, after two days, she'd already gotten used to the guards that surrounded her über important sister. She stared at the man, knowing he looked familiar. Well, more familiar than the others.

"Hello Sexy! You're still alive!" She grinned.

Gabby nicked-named—or named depending how someone looked at it—the guard when she'd been going through the drama with her two mates the previous night. The guys had rejected her sister for some dumb reason. While Gabs had been trying to reaffirm her hotness, she hit on the guard. It'd been all fun and games until Gabriella's mates threatened to rip the man's head off.

The wolf blushed and tugged at the collar of his uniform. "Um, Tor, Miss Wickham. And breakfast has already been ordered. It should be arriving," a low ding from Scarlet's elevator flitted through the room. "Now."

With that, the man disappeared and returned with a massive rolling cart topped with a half-dozen covered plates.

"Oh, I think I love you, Hello Sexy." Scarlet's words were immediately followed by a wince. "Never mind, I hate you with a passion unrivaled." Ah, her mates had to be speaking with her telepathically. "There? Better now?" When no more grumbles from Scarlet came, Whitney figured things were good.

In moments, the Wickhams were settled and munching.

"So…" Scarlet nibbled on the only freaking cheese Danish in the whole pile of food. "I'm not seeing that well-fucked look and you're moving a little too well for a woman who had two sets of wolfy chompers in her shoulder."

"Yeah. We aren't mating until 'they've done some research.'" Whitney swung the air quotes, banana in one hand, squished muffin in the other. Well, brownie, but a muffin—even squished—qualified as breakfast more so than a brownie.

"No boinking? At all?" Gabby was horrified. "You three were on fire when we left. Did they even throw you a bone? Like an orgasm or ten as a consolation prize?"

Whitney shook her head. "Nope. They're concerned about what would happen. Plus, I think they're worried about Sarvis even though they said they're not."

Scarlet nodded. "Yeah, he's evil with a capitol ass and lowercase hat." She tilted her head to the side. "I'm actually surprised you got here. I mean, he shoulda been lying in wait to pounce and steal you away so he could kill you and solve his little problem." She shrugged.

"Are you kidding?" Whitney hadn't thought of that.

"Duh. He's like the evil villain. With all that snarling and yelling about you being handled 'permanently.' Plus that whole abomination thing." Gabby snorted. "Just don't go into any basements. Or bleach your hair blonde. In the movies, it's the dumb blondes who get killed first." Her sister's gaze fell to Whitney's chest. "I'd say don't get a boob job, but they're already big. Yet another movie-inspired strike against you." She sighed and shrugged. "Not much to be done about it now. I'm sure Emmett and Levy won't let him kill you."

"I just… But… I don't know what to…" Whitney was sputtering, but there was so much disbelief and awe bouncing around that she couldn't stop. She shoved her squished muffin into her mouth to keep the incoherent words at bay. Except even then, she managed to shout around the chocolate goodness. "You're talking about me being killed like it's nothing!"

Which hurt. And annoyed her. She wasn't sure which was worse.

58

A familiar baritone cut in. "That's because they care about you and you took a huge risk by leaving your room without your mates." Whitney scrunched her face and squeezed her eyes shut. She hated it when others were right. The cherry on top was that it was a *man* who was right. Ugh.

"Hey, baby," her sister purred at her mate, Keller.

"Ladies." Eyes still closed, she listened as he thumped across the room and then laid a moan-inducing kiss on Scarlet.

"Whitney?" Keller spoke to her.

"Huh?" She wasn't opening her eyes. If she kept them shut, she was invisible. Period.

"I'm sure your mates—"

The building shook, decorations and furniture bounced off the floor and pictures fell from the walls. With the first tremor, her eyes snapped open and the world seemed to move in slow motion. Glass shattered as the wood frames collided with the marble covered ground. A wave of pure, bone-crunching power immediately followed the earthquake. On *its* heels was a roar so loud that whatever hadn't broken, splintered into a million pieces.

Scarlet clung to Keller, his amber eyes boring into Whitney's, while Gabby held onto her chair and miraculously, didn't lose hold of her donut. Whitney held on to her own seat, gripping it tightly as the combination of the trembling building, the intense magic, and deafening roar flowed over her.

"Your mates are awake." Keller yelled over the growing din.

She really wanted to give him the middle finger and scream a great big "duh." True the roars were animalistic and could have been anyone, but she knew without a doubt the source of the drama was her mates.

"Can you tell 'em I'm fine?" She echoed his volume. The man gave her a deadpan look. Ass. "Howl at them or something. Don't you have a werewolf bat-signal?" His expression didn't change. "Seriously? You got nothing?"

Keller rolled his eyes, tilted his head back and let out a howl that nearly shattered her eardrums. He repeated it, a quick, triple yell that finally quieted the building.

When everything settled, the man gave her a small smirk. "You are going to be in so much trouble."

"I have no idea what you're talking about." She sniffed. She'd blaze her way through the coming confrontation. She was a big girl. She could see her sisters if she wanted to and they couldn't say any—

Then they were there, hair sticking up, muscled chest and abs bare, pants barely clinging to their waists, and eyes blazing white. Their magic lurked just below the surface. No hint of amber, no tell-tale signs that the wolf or man were in residence.

Of course, their physical appearance wasn't what shocked her. No, it was the way they hadn't used the stairs. Or the elevator. Or doors in general. They popped into the room *à la* "I Dream of Genie."

One second the room held the guards, the Wickham sisters and Keller and the next, they had two more bodies with them. *Poof.*

"Oh, that's wicked cool." Gabriella's words cut through the room's tension.

"'Wicked cool?' What, you're from Boston all of a sudden?"

"I watched Good Will Hunting." She sighed. "Matt Damon is so hot." Then Gabby rolled her eyes. "I hear you, I hear you. The gorgeous Matt Damon is not hot in any way, shape or form O-glorious Lickable Men." Her sister turned to her with twinkling eyes. "Telepathy, a gift and a curse. It is fun to rile them up now and again." Gabriella's attention switched to Emmett and Levy and pointed at them before returning her attention to Whitney. "Just not that much. 'Cause that is wicked, please don't kill me, scary." Growls from Whitney's mates sent the last few unbroken pieces in the room clattering to the ground. "And now, I'm out."

It was a mass exodus. Guards, Keller, and her sisters were there one second and then they were gone, all of them scrambling for the exits.

"Traitors!" Of course, they didn't hear her because they. Were. Gone.

Which left her with two very pissed off, very large, very powerful wolves.

"Um, hey, you're up." She faked a chuckle and gave them an unsure smile.

"Yes," Levy slowly advanced, his voice a little too calm for her tastes. "We are. And do you know what we woke up to?"

"Um, did they forget your coffee? I distinctly remember ordering coff—"

61

Emmett growled. "You. Were. Gone." With every word, he took a stomping step forward.

Whitney immediately jumped from her seat and put distance between them, hiding behind the chair she'd just occupied. "Now, we can talk about this."

Levy disappeared from the spot before her and reappeared at her back. Strong, fur lined hands gripped her upper arms. Really neat trick.

"We can talk about the fact that we awoke alone? That we thought the worst? That we thought you were dea—" Levy growled and squeezed tighter. "We couldn't find you, Whitney. We can't sense you because we aren't fully mated."

"Which we're going to fix." Emmett approached her, barley contained strength and tension filling his every step. "Now."

"Wait now, let's slow your roll right there. We should talk or… something. You're a little cranky right now—"

Levy nuzzled her, stepped closer and his heat slid through the thin shirt she wore. He aligned his body with hers, shoulders down to knees, and she felt every dip and curve of his muscles. Then there was the thick hardness that fit easily along the cheeks of her ass.

"Cranky is waking up without coffee. This is little beyond cranky." He scraped her neck with his fangs and memories of the previous afternoon assaulted her. The pleasure, pure and sweet, pinged around her brain and she couldn't wait for a repeat. She just hoped the whole intense pain post-orgasm thing didn't come along again.

So engrossed in Levy, she hadn't noticed Emmett's closeness. Not until he dug his fingers into her hair, tightened his hold and forced her to look at him. "This is furious. This is filled with rage. This is fixing the problem so this never happens again."

"Problem?" She tugged against his hold, wincing with the slight sting. "I am *not* a problem, you jerk! I am sweetness and light and the best thing that ever happened to you. Do you hear me? Sweetness and light!"

"Emmett, back off." Levy's order was unmistakable.

"No, she needs to understand the result of her actions." He tugged again and the dim light that surrounded her flared to life with the small pain. She glared at him, matching his anger pound for pound and not caring if the man's eyes were white. She should have feared him, feared the ire, but she didn't bother. She was his mate, it wasn't like he'd really hurt her. Maybe.

"Whitney, Sarvis wants you gone. It's a fact. We sugar coated things, but you know as well as I do that he'd like you six feet under. And if that happened, if you were torn from our lives," Emmett's hold eased, his fingers sliding from her hair to cup her cheek. He stroked her skin with his thumb, the gentle touch so different from the passion in his words. "If you died, the wolves wouldn't survive it."

"Your wolves?" She was worried his answer would be…

"All wolves."

Ouch.

"The moral of the story is: staying alive would be good." She released a small chuckle.

"Yes." Levy released her arms and slid his hands around her waist. "And part of that is mating you. Now. We'll be connected like your sisters are with their mates and no one could ever take you and hide you. We'll be a thought away."

Whitney's heart hurt, a bolt of emotional pain spearing through her. "You only want to mate me to keep me safe. Last night you said…"

"We said a lot of stupid things, but there's no question that you're ours and we're taking you now. We can argue about it later."

"But later I'll be—"

She didn't get a chance to finish. Not when Emmett kissed her. Hell, it wasn't a kiss, it was a possession, a taking. His lips crashed to hers, molding to her mouth and forcing her to submit. Not that she had a problem with that. Especially when he slipped his tongue into her, licked and lapped at her. His flavors, sweetness with a hint of heat, exploded across her tongue.

She moaned into him, letting Levy support her at her waist while she slumped forward against Emmett. She wanted more, she wanted everything. With the rise of her arousal her skin rippled and the glow intensified, the light slipping past her eyelids. She needed his touch, everywhere. Those lips needed to kiss the hundreds of Marks covering his skin. Twice.

Their tongues twined and battled, Emmett stealing control until Whitney snatched it back. She wanted to submit to the large wolf, craved to let him take the lead, but she also didn't want to simply roll over and bare her stomach. She hunted every hint of his flavors, delving deeper, sinking into him and she didn't ever want to leave.

Pushing even closer, she clutched at his shoulders and reveled in the feel of his muscles flush against her, gloried in the thick cock that branded her hip. Regardless of their reasons, she wanted them. They belonged to her and she didn't give a damn about the threat from Sarvis, she wanted to complete their mating.

Whitney yanked her lips from Emmett despite her desire to do anything but keep kissing him. "Bed. Bed bed bed bed." She pressed a hard kiss to his lips. "Bed."

"Coming right up." Levy released her and Emmett swung her up into his arms, cradling her against his chest. He spun and strode toward an open door. A door that led to a bedroom in her *sister's* suite.

Whitney wiggled and fought. "Hell no, I am not mating in a bed I'm sure my sister has fucked in. She's banged those two on nearly every surface, and I'm not risking coming into contact with their biological material."

"Biological material?"

Whitney rolled her eyes and looked at Levy over Emmett's shoulder. "Ex-wet spots. I am not touching those."

The wolf grinned. "You heard the lady, Emmett. No biological material."

Emmett gazed at her, and she returned her attention to the massive wolf holding her. "As my lady wishes. Hold on tight."

She opened her mouth to ask why except the air was sucked from her lungs and blackness invaded her vision. She couldn't even see the now familiar glow of her skin within this… place. Yet, just as quickly as they'd entered the darkness, they emerged into the bedroom they shared. Still snug in Emmett's arms, she pushed and wiggled until the man released her.

"What the fuck was that?" She stumbled and fell back onto the bed.

"That was how we got to you so quickly." The two men advanced on her, Emmett to her right and Levy on her left.

Only… suddenly, Emmett was gone.

"And that is how we…" Gentle lips ghosted over the back of her neck. Levy was still in front of her which meant…" That is how we will always be where you need us."

"I, uh," she shivered. "Need you."

Levy dropped to his knees and eased forward, nudging her thighs apart as he closed the distance between them. Her pussy heated, warming with their nearness and what was to come.

"Oh, sweet, you need us more than you know." Callused hands stroked her legs, sliding over her calves, past her knees and then to the tops of her thighs. "You need us desperately." Those palms continued their journey, easing toward her aching center. "Urgently." His fingers traced where her thighs met her hips, his thumbs dipping down and so damned close to her wet, panty-clad slit she wanted to cry. "Your pussy is begging for us."

The words wrapped around her, stroked her, and sent her arousal higher. Each syllable plucked her nipples and kneaded her breasts. Wait, those were real hands, Emmett's hands. She moaned and allowed her head to drop back to rest on the wolf's shoulder. Yes, she loved their touch. Every word that fell from Levy's mouth was true. Every. Single. One.

She whimpered and tilted her hips, hoping to force him where she desired him most. Emmett continued to tease her through the T-shirt she still wore. Every tug on her nipples went straight to her clit forcing the bundle of nerves to pulse. Her pussy clenched, tightening on air and she knew that in moments she would be filled by one of their cocks. But whose?

Screw it, she didn't really care. One of her mates would slip into her wet cunt, and the other would ease into her ass. They'd take her, thrust in and out of her, until they came together and sank their teeth into her flesh. They'd be tied as one then. Forever and ever and fuck you Sarvis if he tried to tear them apart.

Then her thoughts scattered. Blown to bits when Levy's thumbs finally came in contact with her sex lips, he stroked and pet her through the thin fabric of her wet panties. Up and down he teased her slit, the fabric blunting the sensation, but still giving her pleasure.

She moaned and rocked against his touch. "Levy."

The annoying man chuckled. "Yes, sweet? Is there something you needed?"

Whitney whimpered. "Touch me."

"Oh, I'm touching you. So is Emmett. We've both got our hands on you."

Stupid cocky man. "But," she whined.

Those thumbs traced the laced edge of her panties, tips dipping beneath the trim and stroking her soaked heat. "This what you want?"

Whitney rocked and wiggled, fighting for more from Levy while she arched her back and pushed her breasts firmer against Emmett's palms. "Please please please."

"I think you should give her what she wants, Levy." Emmett traced her ear with his tongue and the caress sent a shudder through her body straight to her pussy.

She nodded. "Yes, what he said."

Levy, her sweet, caring Levy gave her an evil grin. "I'll think about it." With a wink, his attention turned back to the juncture of her thighs, his gaze firmly centered on his hands. He tormented and teased her, fingers dipping behind the fabric and petting her soaked pussy before retreating once again.

"If you don't gimme what I want, I swear I'll... I'll do something really mean and horrible and please touch me!"

Warm breath bathed her inner thigh and Levy lapped at her skin, pressing a soft kiss to her heated flesh. "You just had to ask, sweet." He licked her and caught some of her skin between his teeth. The blunted sting sent another bolt of pleasure through her and she moaned. "Sit still."

She whimpered, determined to do as he asked. Beneath her gaze, his hand shifted. Like, it truly went from manly fingers to werewolf claws. Thin, pale nails became thick and black while skin gave way to pale fur. If she hadn't been so aroused and needy, she would have been horrified. Okay, maybe not horrified, but it would have freaked her out a little.

But when the sound of tearing fabric hit the air—immediately followed by the coolness of the room fanning her slick pussy—she didn't give a damn. Because then he was touching her. A single finger (thankfully human) teased the seam of her sex lips, tracing the line up and then down again, gathering more and more cream with every pass.

"Oh God, please…" Another great wrench of fabric and the chilled air bathed her breasts, the T-shirt she wore now shredded and hanging off her in tatters. She was bare before them, plump curves exposed to them both, and she cringed.

Whitney lifted her arms to cover herself, embarrassment and self-doubt assaulting her more and more for every second she was revealed. Only… only her arms were held captive by Emmett, his embrace forcing her to remain still. Levy kept his position between her thighs and his gaze held nothing but desire.

The blue she loved alternated and shifted from blue to amber to white and then cycled again. But his thoughts were easily read in his gaze.

He wanted her. "So beautiful."

"Gorgeous."

"Ours."

"Levy. Emmett," she whispered and squirmed.

Levy eased forward, and his breath fanned over her flesh, sending goose bumps racing up her spine. He stopped a hairsbreadth from where she wanted him most.

"Do you need him, love?" Emmett's voice was barely more than a growl in her ear.

"Y-Yes." She did. So, so, gimme-gimme bad.

"What do you need?" His words vibrated through her.

"Tell me what you want, Whitney." The air puffed across her swollen lower lips.

"Lick me," she whispered, but the wolves had no problem hearing her.

Levy stuck his tongue out and flicked the top of her slit. "Here?"

She nodded.

"Words, sweet."

She moaned and dropped her head back against Emmett's shoulder. "Please lick my pussy."

"Aw, sweet, you just had to ask."

A millisecond later, she was insanely glad she'd asked. Levy didn't hesitate to give her what she desired. The moment the last syllable dripped from his lips, he made love to her.

Levy pressed her legs wider with his hands, gripping her inner thighs with tender pressure and she let him do as he wished. Those teasing thumbs eased her sex lips apart, exposing her to his gaze.

"I don't think I've ever seen anything so beautiful." His tone was filled with awe.

Whitney opened her mouth to tell him her pussy wasn't exactly the Mona Lisa, but then her world was wrapped in a haze of pleasure.

The wolf between her thighs licked her from the very center of her heat to her clit and back again. One long lap after another, he bathed her in bliss. Again and again, circling her needy opening and then on to the bundle of nerves that made her moan with pleasure.

"Levy. Need." She couldn't even form complete sentences.

And Emmett wasn't a passive partner. He continued his seductive assault on her breasts while his mouth, that talented mouth, licked, nipped and sucked on her skin. Even more, the wicked words that tumbled from his lips merely sent her blazing hotter.

"Do you like his tongue? Do you like the way he laps at your pretty pussy?"

Said pussy clenched, tightening and sending yet another jolt of pleasure through her veins. The men were going to burn her from the inside out. Now she understood why her sisters screamed all night and had goofy smiles all day.

"He's going to make you come and then I'm going to slide my cock into you, love. Do you want that?" He captured the flesh of her shoulder between his teeth and bit down. A spear of pain ricocheted through her.

"Yes."

"You want to come on my cock?"

Levy moaned against her pussy and flicked her clit while a blunt fingertip circled her entrance. Oh, God, circled and then pushed forward, easing into her sheath. She rocked her hips, tilting them in an effort to get him deeper and he allowed her to snatch that bit of control from him. Then his

71

mouth latched on to the pleasurable bundle of nerves near the top of her slit.

"Yes." The word came out with a breathy rasp.

"Then you have to come for your mate."

That she could totally do. Especially when that single finger was joined by another, stretching her sheath wide. His tongue picked up a steady rhythm, flicking her clit while he added the tiniest bit of suction to his actions.

"Uh-huh." She tilted her head to the side, encouraging Emmett's wanderings while she focused entirely on the sensations caused by the man between her thighs. She moaned and groaned with his every move. He licked, she whimpered. He sucked, she sighed. It went round and round, her body reacting to him and him reacting to her sounds.

Those thick fingers plunged in and out of her, the pads sliding over her G-spot with every pass and his mouth never lost its rhythm. Yes, that was what she needed. She needed the constant stimulation to shove her toward the edge of her release.

With every whispered word, nibble of her neck, and torturous caress to her pussy, she neared her climax. Her nipples hardened further and her pussy clenched and milked Levy's invading fingers.

Whitney's body trembled, her peak now looming before her. The pleasure was gathering, growing and expanding into an ever increasing bubble and any second now...

A tiny flick of pain invaded her increasing bliss, and that was all she needed. Her body reacted to the small ache by pouring pure, unadulterated ecstasy into her veins. She screamed with her release, body reacting so violently that she wrenched herself from Emmett's arms. She arched, head thrown back as she roared. Flaring light filled the room, illuminating every nook and cranny as her body succumbed to Levy and Emmett's ministrations.

Lava, hot and pure, washed through her, setting her nerves on fire and it added to the bliss of her release. Whitney's muscles trembled, twitching, and jerking as wave after wave of ecstasy assaulted her. Hell, even her toes curled and that definitely hadn't ever happened before. His tongue flicked, fingers sliding in and out of her wet pussy and all she could do was ride the wave, enjoy the blissful torment.

Levy didn't pause in his torture. He continued his pace while her body burst into flames, and she couldn't have cared less. Not when she had them surrounding her. Not when she had them to keep her safe. Not when she had them to make her come a million times over the coming years.

When she couldn't take any more, she reached for him, sliding her fingers through his hair and tugging on the blond strands. "Levy." He sucked hard and glanced her clit with his fang once again. "Oh, God, Levy stop."

She was sobbing, and she didn't give a damn. It felt glorious and painful in equal measure. Part of her screamed for him to cease so she could breathe. The other part of her told her other half to shut the fuck up, she was coming, damn it.

Eventually—finally?—he eased his attentions, slowing his fingers and tongue until his touch barely registered. Whitney's breath continued in heaving pants and the twitches and jerks kept randomly slipping through her, but at least she could think again.

Think about Levy.

And about Emmett.

And about having them both inside her.

Like, now.

*

Eyes locked on Whitney, Levy slipped his fingers free of her soaked pussy and brought them to his mouth. Craving even more of her taste, he lapped and licked the digits, savoring the salty musk of her juices. His mate blushed at his actions, red suffusing her cheeks. He wondered if she'd always be quick to embarrass.

He released his fingers with a low pop. "Delicious, sweet."

With ease, he rolled to his feet, hardened cock bobbing within the confines of his thin pants, begging for the feel of her wrapped around his dick. He gripped his shaft through the fabric and stroked himself, shuddering with the blunted friction.

Emmett shifted, and he turned his attention to his fellow Warden as he spoke to Whitney. "Are you ready to be ours, love?"

Already his friend had it bad.

Whitney squirmed, reddening further. "I haven't… I, uh… I mean, I have, but…"

His partner growled, wrapping his arms around their mate and he cupped her mound. "You've never had a man in this delicious pussy and ass at the same time."

She whimpered, and a blush filled her entire body. "No."

"Damn, sweet." Levy growled, the wolf thrilling at the fact they'd be the only ones to possess that part of her. His shaft throbbed and hardened further while a drop of pre-cum formed at the tip, wetting his pajamas. "Need you."

He looked over Whitney's shoulder and met Emmett's gaze, communicating without words. It was time. After long moments, the wolf finally nodded.

He held his hand out for her, noting the tremble of her fingers as she gripped him. Before she rose, Emmett stroked her pussy and that slight tremble turned into a violent shudder.

Levy tugged and she stumbled into him, her lush curves fitting against him as if she'd been made to cradle his body. Then again, she had.

"That feel good, sweet?"

She whimpered and wiggled against him, testing his resolve even further. He was going to come inside her, fill her with his scent as he bit and claimed her forever.

Distantly he knew Emmett moved around the room, stripping before he headed to the bedside table and retrieved the bottle of lube that had come with the room. The hotel staff had stocked the suites well.

"Are you ready, Whitney?" He brushed her tattered shirt from her shoulders then reached around her and stroked her back, sliding along her spine until he got to the crack of her ass. He didn't stop there. No, he delved farther until her warmth met his fingertips. Between those cheeks lay heaven.

"Are you ready for me to push my cock into your ass? It's going to feel so good. So tight for me."

Emmett's growl snared their attention. Yeah, they'd talked about how they'd eventually take her, Levy in her pussy, taking her face-to-face, while Emmett enjoyed her ass. But the man had hidden himself from her long enough. He generally growled and snarled and had never been one to do well with women. His partner was a man of action and not pretty words.

Well, it was time for Whitney to see the softer side of her other mate.

"Please?"

"You want me in your ass?" Levy smirked when Emmett glared at him.

"Yes," she hissed when his fingertip glanced her dark hole.

He could practically hear the other wolf's curses and internal snarls. Not that it mattered. Emmett was head over heels for their mate and would do as she desired.

With a smirk, he nudged Whitney toward the bed. "In the middle, hands and knees."

Without hesitating, she did as he directed, crawling into place, hands planted firmly on the soft mattress and ass and pussy fully exposed to him. Levy quickly shed his pants and then eased behind her. He held out his hand, grinning when the bottle was slapped onto his palm hard enough to cause a little sting. "Emmett, why don't you get under our mate and lick her little clit while I get her ready." He popped the top, noting the little shiver that traveled over her body in a wave. "And, sweet, feel free to suck his cock."

76

It took a few moments of shifting bodies to get into position, but then he had them both where he wanted them. He'd never taken the lead so firmly before and he was finding he liked it. A lot.

Levy drizzled some of the viscous fluid along the crease of Whitney's ass, smiling when she moaned around Emmett's cock. He didn't care why she made the arousing sound, he was simply happy they could give their mate pleasure.

Squirting a little of the lube over his fingers, he tossed the bottle aside and got to the task of preparing their mate. He stroked her lower back, acclimating her to his touch while he teased her back hole with his fingertip. He circled and danced over her forbidden entrance, smiling at the sounds she made. Each one had his cock hardening and lengthening farther.

When he breached her with a single digit, she tilted her hips and exposed even more of that lush ass to his gaze. He gently thrust in and out of her until he moved with ease, and then he added another.

His balls were ready to burst in anticipation, cock dribbling a steady stream of pre-cum. *Soon. Very, very soon.*

Two fingers became three, Whitney's volume increasing with his every touch, his every stroke and caress. Her ass rippled and clenched his invading fingers, signaling their mate had another orgasm rushing forward. Yes, she'd come again. While they were inside her.

With as thick as his cock was, three digits became four, his pace increasing and matching the hums and moans that came from her perfect mouth. Now Emmett joined in the music of her sounds, his grunts and groans battling hers.

Yeah, having his partner beneath her had been a good idea. Having the other male take her pussy first was even better.

Sure he'd stretched her sufficiently, he eased his fingers free of her, smiling when she wiggled her ass. Smiling wider when she popped off Emmett's cock and glared at him over her shoulder while that plump ass swayed once again.

"It's time, sweet."

Whitney melted for him, an emotion so close to his own sliding across her gaze.

It took mere moments to change positions, Levy flopping to his back and motioning for Whitney to come forward. "Come, sweet."

"I thought Emmett was going in my…" She blushed so bright he thought the white glow that came from her would suddenly turn red.

"Trust me." He wiggled his fingers and she did as asked, crawling toward him. But when she went to straddle his hips, he stopped her. "Turn around." She gave him a puzzled frown, but again, listened, presenting him with her back and a perfect view of her lush ass. Then she squeaked when he positioned his cock against her back hole. "Now, you're in control. Take me and lay back and we'll do the rest, sweet." When she hesitated, he reinforced his desires. "Take my cock, Whitney."

Small hands rested on his thighs as she leaned forward, but then he didn't give a damn what she did. Not when she eased onto his dick, the tip popping past that first ring of muscle and pure pleasure and scorching heat surrounded him. She paused, and he took a moment to soothe her, hands tracing some of the swirling marks that decorated her pale skin. She moved again, taking more of his cock and he pulsed within her.

"Good, sweet. Take more." He pushed the words past gritted teeth. She was so close to having all of him. "A little more."

"Burns," she whined.

"But feels good, doesn't it?"

She stilled, and a second ticked by but then she nodded.

"So take the rest."

And she did. She pushed and sank over him until his cock was completely enmeshed in her forbidden heat.

"Damn, you're tight." He turned to Emmett. "Just think about how tight her cunt is going to be." She gasped and her pussy clenched, causing her ass to do the same. Oh yes, his mate liked a little dirty talk. "Do you want that? Emmett in your cunt while I'm in your ass?"

She nodded again.

Levy looked to his fellow Warden, noted the man's feral need and the way he rapidly tugged on his dick. "What are you waiting for Emmett? Our mate needs you."

The man eased closer, stalking him and Whitney like the wolf that lived inside him. Emmett knelt between their spread thighs, leaving Levy's sight, but he could imagine his partner's movements and he did what he could to speed the initial taking along. As soon as Emmett slipped inside Whitney, all of his friend's hesitation would flee.

Gripping Whitney's shoulders, gritting his teeth against the need to come, he eased her backward. "Lay back on me, sweet. Show Emmett the pussy that belongs to him."

The change in position sent a lightning bolt of pleasure down his spine, caressing him from inside out, and he couldn't wait to come inside her.

Now he could see Emmett, see the emotions that flitted across his long-time friend's face. Worry. Love. Anxiousness. Love. Need. Love.

Levy spread his legs wider. "Come on, man, our mate needs us."

"Need need need." She panted and rocked her hips.

The other Warden's eyes flared white and the color stuck, that part of him coming out to play. "Mine."

There was suddenly no distance that separated them, no air that lurked between their bodies. A slight pressure, a tightening of her ass against his cock was the only hint that Emmett was with them. *With* them.

Thank God because he was *so* ready to come.

*

Emmett was gonna come. Fuck, he only had the head of his cock inside her snug pussy, and already her body was easing him toward release. Hell no, easing was too timid a word for what she did to him.

Whitney burned him.

He closed his eyes, savoring the sensations of sinking into her silken heat. He eased in and then retreated, feeding her pussy more and more of his length with every entrance. He wouldn't last. Not with the way she gripped him, tightened and milked him.

His wolf howled in joy, overwhelmed with happiness at their impending mating. This was it. Apparently they'd half-assed this earlier, but now it was on purpose with pure, selfish intent. He wanted to get it done before she realized she'd made a bad bargain by mating him. He wasn't soft and sweet like Levy. He growled and snarled and—

A stinging pinch came from his left arm. His eyes snapped open and he gazed at an angry, passion-glazed Whitney.

"When you're fucking me, it'd be nice of you to *be* with me." Fury tinted her words.

Pain suffused his heart and he stilled, his cock fully embed in her soaking wet pussy. "I'm not... I..." He leaned down, blanketed her body with his own and pressed his forehead to hers. "I'm not like Levy."

She stroked his face and cupped his cheek. "Of course you're not."

"I can't be sweet and gentle."

"I know."

"I don't want to scare you. The things I want..."

Whitney rubbed her thumb along his cheek bone. "And I want them, too. You're mine, Emmett. I have sweet behind me. Give me you. Give me everything."

"Whitney…"

His mate closed the small distance between their lips and brushed a kiss across his mouth, licking at the seam and then slipping into him. Her flavors, the sweetness and warmth, washed over his tongue. It spurred his wolf, his *other*, into action. He couldn't hold back any longer. Not when she was giving permission and enticing him to give her all of him.

Emmett's hips moved of their own volition, sliding out of her clinging heat and in again. He savored the pleasure that surrounded his dick, the bliss that tugged at his balls as he pumped in and out of her.

His pace started gentle, easing her into a rhythm that would drive them all wild. With their position, Levy was a passive partner. But based on his sounds, the man had no trouble with laying back and enjoying the ride.

He dug his hands into the mattress beneath them, his fingers shifting into claws and piercing the soft surface. They'd definitely have a few additions to the hotel bill.

Whitney's small hands gripped his shoulders, human nails stabbing his flesh, driving him wild with the added hint of pain. He picked up his pace, slamming their hips together in a lewd rhythm of flesh hitting flesh. The sounds of their meeting bodies filled the room, the echoes joined by their combined moans and groans.

Her pussy clung to him, tightening and releasing in a fierce milking beat. Their kiss continued, and she sucked his tongue, the sensation going straight to his cock. It twitched and pulse in time with her actions, shoving him closer to release. His balls pulled up high and tight against his body, hardening in preparation of emptying himself in his mate.

She'd be his soon. Theirs.

Pleasure raced along his spine, the ecstasy sliding through him with ease, and a shudder overtook his body. Fuck, his dick hurt and felt blissful at the same time. He wanted to come, but didn't want the torment to end.

He shoved back his orgasm, concentrating instead on the kiss they shared, on the hardened nipples brushing his chest, and on the whimpers that transferred from her mouth to his.

"Harder, man." Levy released a harsh groan.

Whitney pulled back enough to speak against his lips. "Please. Please, Emmett. Mate."

The word, the admission on her lips, was enough to drive the wolf and the *other* mad. His beast roared forward, the crack and crunch of reforming bones warring with the sounds of their sex. Fur pushed through his pores to coat his arms and chest.

"Yes, claim me, my wolf."

He went insane. Pounding into her heat, eyes locked on the pulse that beat beneath the skin of her throat. The wolf wanted her blood flowing over its tongue. Because that'd mean she belonged to them then. Theirs, theirs, theirs.

"Come for me first." The words were barely intelligible, but the flare of light emanating from her body was not.

Her eyes bore into his and he was transfixed by the paling of the orbs. He didn't understand the ramifications of mating Whitney, didn't know what would happen to her, but he didn't believe fate would give them a mate if it'd harm her. Well, harm her further.

He plunged into her, shaking the bed with his force and she gasped his name. "Emmett…"

"Like that?" He repeated the thrust, sending the headboard banging against the wall. They'd have to pay for that too.

"Please. Levy, make him—"

Levy couldn't make him do anything. He chuckled, but picked up his pace anyway, anxious for her to come on his dick so he could come inside her. With every entrance, her pussy clenched, seemed to beg for his cum.

Soon. He'd give it to her soon.

Whitney writhed between them, body shifting and jerking and he knew her orgasm was within reach.

"Rub her clit, man." Emmett grunted when she tightened and knotted around him.

He felt Levy's hand snake between them and recognized the instant his partner found that little nub. Hell, the whole hotel knew when he found what he'd been hunting. Their mate screamed to the heavens, their names on her lips.

The regular pulsing of her cunt grew sporadic and uneven and he knew. She was there, right on the edge. "Damn it, come, love."

Her gaze focused on his, only it was purely, completely Whitney's *other*. It peered at him, strengthening and soothing him in equal measure and he recognized himself in her gaze.

Another, primal scream echoed in the room and a rush of power consumed him. Their mate lit up like a blazing star and it was enough to shove him over the edge. His cock gave a violent shudder and then it was there. Pure bliss surrounded his balls and squeezed, and he could do nothing but listen to his body's desires.

He came with a shuddering roar, pumping his hips jerkily against Whitney's and he vaguely recognized Levy doing the same. Their cocks slid against one another, the thin tissues of her pussy and ass separating them. Yet he felt his friend come, felt the man pulse inside her.

He met Levy's eyes and with unspoken agreement they struck.

Emmett sank his wolf's canines into Whitney's left shoulder, teeth slicing through her skin and flesh with ease. Pure, coppery-tinged ambrosia flowed over his tongue. His beast howled with the first hint, reveling in the final claiming of their mate. They were tied together with unbreakable bonds now. Both inside and out she was bound to them.

Then he felt it. The *other* shoved forward, pushed itself past the wolf and into Whitney. His power met Levy's and jointly, the magic of their wolves filled their mate. A blinding, white light suffused his eyelids, burning into his eyes with the intensity.

The swell grew and grew until it consumed them. Nothing could be seen beyond the glow of their entwined bodies. One thought became another and another and he couldn't tell his mental words from Whitney's and Levy's.

This went past the physical claiming of wolf and woman. The ties were soul deep and he knew, instinctively, that only death would ever part them. Eventually, the light dimmed and he opened his eyes, blinking away the bright spots that clouded his vision.

A barely-there thought flitted to him, pleasure tainted by pain, and he immediately slowed the suction and eased his teeth from Whitney's shoulder while Levy did the same. The scent of her blood filled the room, battling with the musky flavors of their sex.

Emmett lapped at his mark, smug over the fact the bite would scar and every wolf would know she was claimed.

"Bastard." Whitney's words were slurred and garbled but still understandable. As were her emotions. He realized they'd shared hints of this exchange before, but now he read her without any effort at all.

Which meant she could also sense his feelings.

"Sticky." She moaned and wiggled. "They were right. Threesome sex *is* squishy."

Emmett chuckled and placed one last kiss to her shoulder. He eased back, shifting his weight and slowly pulling free of her clinging pussy. He wanted to remain buried inside her forever, but he had to admit, he was feeling rather sticky himself.

Disregarding her whines, he left her and went to the bathroom, anxious to get a washcloth to clean their mate. Levy could get his own if he wanted one.

"Asshole!"

Yeah, well, he didn't care. Mate first.

"Aw," Whitney sighed. "See? You can be sweet."

He reentered the room and rolled his eyes. The two of them now lay on their side, Whitney facing him and giving him a gorgeous view of her curves.

Her no longer glowing curves. Not a hint of light seeped from her pores.

His mate stilled and looked down at her body. "You're right!" She pushed up and then looked over her shoulder. He easily sensed her frustration and annoyance. "Get your dick out of my ass. I gotta see myself and I can't do that with a telephone pole inside me."

Now he felt Levy's cockiness. *Dick.*

Why yes, my dick is inside her.

"You want it in there ever again? Get it out now."

His partner harrumphed, but did as she demanded. A small wince flitted across her features, but it disappeared as quickly as it had arrived.

The moment she was free, she scrambled to her feet and then froze. "Ew, really, really squishy." She held out her hand. "Gimme. I love you guys, but this is seriously gross."

The room stilled, time suspended, and even Whitney had a look of surprise on her face. Seconds ticked by, her words sinking into them all, but then he felt it. He felt the pure truth through the connection they'd formed during the mating. There were no secrets between them. There never could be.

"Whitney..." Emotion clogged Levy's throat and Emmett realized he'd be the one to say it back.

"Whitney. Love." He dropped the damp washcloth and reached for her, pulling her into his arms. Her curves were perfect against him. "We love you, too. So, so much. It's fast and we have so many things to talk about and learn, but it's there. At least the first bit and we'll—"

And then all hell broke loose.

CHAPTER FIVE

Whitney wasn't sure what had happened to her during their mating. At some point there were bright lights. At the time, and all she could think about was some short, older lady telling her not to go into the light. Then she realized she wasn't Carol Anne and she wasn't starring in a remake of Poltergeist. Plus, she was pretty sure Poltergeist wasn't a porn vid.

But the mating details didn't matter because she now stood with a wide-eyed Emmett who was babbling about the two men loving her, and her heart was about to burst. She reached for the cloth, more than ready to rid herself of the "squishy" in favor of the whole "love profession" part of the day. Of course that idea had to be bashed to the ground.

There was no sexy meeting of lips and then awkward after-sex wipe up.

Nope, she got old dudes raiding her room.

The double doors slammed open, intricately carved panels banging against the walls. The collision sent a shower of drywall raining onto the carpet. And within the doorway stood a man she'd never wanted to see again bracketed by four, equally old guys.

And she was naked. Damn it, why did crap have to go down while she was naked?

In a blink, Levy stood before her, blocking her view of the men and Emmett immediately joined him. Well, apparently they didn't care about being naked, but she sure as hell did. Leaning over, she tugged on a sheet, yanking and pulling on the damn thing with all of her might. When it didn't come free, she realized her might was very small.

One last, giant wrench and she had the fabric free. It came loose so suddenly that she thumped to the ground and sprawled on the carpeted floor. *Damn it.* She looked around and realized attentions were still on her guys and not on her lovely display of bedroom acrobatics. Good.

Whitney pushed to her feet and wrapped the sheet around her a few times, tucking the ends within the folds so it would stay up on its own. Dressed-ish, she focused on the men who had killed her squishy buzz.

Sarvis was front and center, rage etched in every saggy feature. His eyes weren't the mud brown that she'd seen the previous day, but were now a dirty cream whereas her mate's always shined a brilliant white. This guy had magic, but it looked...

Tainted. Levy's voice floated through her head.

That seemed right.

So, Sarvis was the head old guy and if the colors of his eyes went along with his power, he didn't seem like he'd be much of a threat. Why were her mates hanging back? She wanted the old guys gone. Finite. Kaput.

Not that easy. He has friends and they know we won't leave you vulnerable long enough to take care of them. They'll go after you, Whitney. It would be best if you stayed alive. Damn, that was the most words she'd ever heard Emmett speak. If telepathy counted as speaking.

And, hey, she wanted to stay alive, too. They were all on the same page with that. *Go Team Living!*

"Sarvis." Yeah, that was the Emmett she knew and loved.

The Elder pinched his lips until they formed a white slash across his face. "You did it, didn't you? I smell the filth of your mating. You had to ruin everything and mate with that *thing.*"

Levy growled, the sound scaring even her.

Sarvis didn't look the least bit worried. "Enough," he snapped, but Levy kept the threat rolling through the room and the old man had to speak over her mate. "You don't understand what you've done. The five families have sacrificed so much to be where we are today. Blood of our forefathers went into changing the spells and altering memories of the Warden Born and your actions have undone it all. You're ruining it with this *woman.*"

He might have just said "whore."

Which she wasn't, thank you very much.

"How is finding a mate wrong, Sarvis?" Emmett seemed to swell in size, and she held her breath.

Shit.

After receiving the "invitation" to the Gathering, Whitney and her sisters had gotten down with the research. Books were re-read, they hopped on the World Wide Werewolf Web and generally gobbled up any information about wolves they could. Some of that info included details on Wardens. Like the fact Wardens could be man, wolf, and then a freaky

91

middle of the road form. It was that half-shift that spawned werewolf legends.

They became the scariest beasts imaginable. Muscles thickened and bulged while their height topped seven feet. Fingers turned into massive, deadly claws and their faces froze into a shape that was a cross between human and beast. Even their feet sported vicious nails. One kick and a person would be gutted.

"*How is finding a mate wrong?*" He repeated his question. "Is it because it proves the laws are wrong?" Her larger mate sneered. "Who decided Wardens were not to mate? Who decided single wolves couldn't be with humans? Who thought they had the *right* to—"

"The five families, that's who!" Energy crackled in the room and the hairs on her arms stood on end. "We made this culture. We made wolves what they are today. The laws exist for a reason."

Levy shook his head. "There can never be a good reason to deny wolves their mates, Sarvis. I love you like a father, but you're wrong."

A soft breeze blew through the room, sending her impromptu dress swaying. The head asshole wasn't pulling that particular string, so who was? Whitney absently listened to the three men arguing as she surveyed the other pissed off jerks.

One after another met her gaze, hate in every one of their dirty milk hued eyes. So much disgust and they didn't even know her. The hatred had damaged them. She knew that just as well as she knew her name.

Her attention shifted to the man to the right of Sarvis. He was tinged with loathing, but his concentration was focused on her. Another breeze came, this one stronger than the last.

Whitney tuned back into the conversation-slash-yelling match. "The Warden Born will destroy you both. In the past, every one of them have. They take and take and give nothing back. Just like every human in the world." Sarvis pointed at her men. "The only reason the Alphas retained their mates is because those men are strong enough to keep their women in check."

She snorted. Let 'em try that with Scarlet and Gabby.

The quintet focused on her. Oh. That sucked.

"We'll rid you of her and her taint. The pain of losing her will fade and then you'll realize how much better off you are." He focused on Levy. "You have to see I'm right."

Another gust of wind slapped her and she realized the internal weather wasn't affecting anyone else. As if the guy only focused his power on her.

She poked Emmett. He needed to pay attention to the X-man Storm wannabe. "Hey, babe."

He grunted and nudged her a step back.

She narrowed her eyes. "Really—"

Another push, this one harder than the last.

Seriously?

This time, she poked Levy. He'd listen. "Hon."

Again with the nudging.

They so aren't getting sex.

"Do you see how she already weakens you?"

"You mentioned Warden Born, Sarvis." Levy's voice was low and held a calm she knew was meant to deceive. "Who are they?"

Sarvis glared. "You won't ever give up."

Hell no her men wouldn't.

The Elder glance behind him and she noted the nods that came his way. Damn it. "I want you to realize that it's your Warden Born who is killing you now."

That sounded really, really bad. Especially since that gentle breeze the freaky guy had been tossing around slowly picked up speed. This time, a nudge wasn't gonna be their answer.

"Uh, guys?" They grunted and she realized their bodies were twisting and turning, bones cracking, crunching and reforming into that grotesque, yet oddly attractive, form. "Guys, really. The old dude is about to pull a Storm on us and I don't think I'd look good all charred from lightning and stuff."

Growls echoed around her, various baritones bouncing off the walls, and she shoved down the fear that assaulted her. She had to be strong for them. There was no way they'd let her get hurt and they didn't need some whiny, cry-baby holding them back.

The old dudes ripped at their clothes, bodies shifting and morphing much like her mates. No, not like her mates.

Where Levy and Emmett hovered in their middle forms, the Elders dropped to all fours and became wolves.

They have the knowledge to take these forms, but not the power. Even Emmett's mental voice was sexy.

The moment Sarvis's wolf feet hit the ground, the man launched at Emmett, jaws wide and teeth snapping at her mate. He easily batted the man aside, only to have Sarvis attack again, the man fighting to injure him.

Levy was in the same boat, one of Sarvis's lackeys attacking her mate again and again.

But the other three… The wind picked up. No, not just picked up, it became a raging cyclone. It spun and twirled, sending glasses and lamps shattering against the walls. She looked around hunting for the wolf causing the damage and found him with ease. He sat hunched in a corner, his eyes glazed and covered with that sickly film of his power.

Whitney growled, snarled, at the cowardly wolf. Something inside her wanted to bite and tear at that wolf's flesh. He fought the Ruling Wardens like a coward, taking part in ganging up on their rulers but from afar. He needed to die. *Yes*, part of her said. He should. They were all cowards, but that one…

A howl yanked her attention back to her mates, back to Emmett who battled Sarvis while another wolf clung to his leg. The bastard had his teeth buried in her mate's thigh, tugging and pulling on his flesh. Blood flowed down Emmett's leg in a steady stream.

No. No no no.

Lightning struck near her right foot, slamming into the concrete and sending shards flying. Vaguely she recognized snippets of pain but then Levy snarled and she was drawn to his struggle. Power or not, enhanced strength or not, injuries still hurt and her connection to them told her that the pain was blunting their magic.

Another howl. More blood. The earth trembled, the cracking of concrete filled the room.

Something inside her wanted out. Out out out. It knew how to protect itself. It knew how to protect its mates. It was Whitney, yet not. It was bred from the marks, yet not.

Warden. Born. The words were strained, but undoubtedly Levy's.

Fate wouldn't have given the Ruling Wardens a mate who couldn't handle their bodies, their wolves, *and* their power.

Whitney rubbed her palms on the sheet that barely clung to her body and delved inside herself. Something lurked, waiting to pounce, but instead she coaxed it forward, held out an ethereal hand and begged it for help.

A sudden rush, an overflowing attack of power assaulted her in that instant and every hint of air left her body.

Oh shit.

She was Day Glo again. The Marks on her body burned, etching into her skin in deep, black lines that contrasted with her pale flesh. The white glow that came from within her was no longer white, but the burning red of her rage.

As if the Earth itself fed her, she drank in power and magic, gorging herself on the seemingly never ending well that presented itself. It was good and pure and so fucking delicious.

Whitney.

Whitney!

God damn it, Whitney! Stop!

She opened eyes she hadn't realized she'd closed and saw the problem immediately. Her mates were pale, worn, the feelings coming from them tinged with exhaustion. Shit. Shit. Shit.

Sarvis noticed their fatigue and attacked again, teeth bared and headed for Emmett's throat.

Hell no.

Whitney raced forward, arm outstretched, and she went from thirty feet away to none, her hand clenched around the wolf's furred throat. "No. Bad puppy." He growled and she shook him side to side. "I said no."

He went into action, fighting for all he was worth, jaws snapping, feet scraping and clawing at air. But she didn't release him. No, he wasn't getting away.

A yelp came from her left, the sound so much like Levy…

Sarvis took advantage of her inattention. While she looked to her mate, he clawed her, nails sinking into the flesh of the arm that held him still.

"You fucking *bastard*."

The next moments played out in slow motion. The magic she'd gathered swelled in her chest, growing, and then it struck. She watched it in awe, a whip of her power sprung from her fingertips and attacked with one task in mind: kill Sarvis.

It hit once, and then again, and then a third time. Each one sliced off a layer of fur and skin, sinking down to his bones. With every strike, his mind opened to her and memories sprung forward, visions of the atrocities he'd witnessed and of the times he'd participated in the horrors. The doctored history of the wolves. The way the five families had perverted everything… Spells changed, twisted, and turned until they adhered to what the families desired.

She was Warden Born, placed on the Earth to mate two Wardens. Her path was only to be revealed once she met her mates. The five families had buried that secret.

They'd bled five females from their own lines—five, mated Warden Born—to corrupt the Gathering spell. The Wardens mated to those females had been murdered in their own beds.

Those single wolves… The five families erased memories and rewrote history. There was nothing keeping them from mating humans. Nothing.

Oh, he so had to die.

Whitney struck harder, furious at the man, his family, his very life. She gloried in the blood, the carnage, and ached to taste his lifeblood on her tongue.

Okay, wait. That grossed her out and she threw up a little bit.

That loss in concentration was all it took for her to lose hold of her power and it fled from her command as quickly as it'd come. The magic drained from her, sliding back to Levy and Emmett in a rushing wave that left her exhausted.

But Sarvis was dead. Go team.

Low growls remained in the room, the crunch and crack of bone immediately followed by soft whimpers, and Whitney spun. She sought her mates, relieved to find them still standing not far away. They each fought a single wolf, one of the other five dead at Emmett's feet.

But that left one…

A definitive snap followed immediately by another signaled two wolves' deaths. Four down.

She let her gaze sweep the room, the bloodthirsty part of her more than ready to feast once again. Ugh. Feast. Ew.

Oh, but then something moved and caught her eye. No, *he* moved. That thing inside her, the *other*, stirred and she didn't hesitate. Whitney bolted across the space, flying over the ground and right at the lame X-man wannabe. She practically tasted his blood on her tongue, the coppery tang flowing over her taste-buds and—

"Whitney." Massive arms swept her up and she found herself plastered against Emmett's chest. She screeched and clawed at her mate's hold. He was so cock-blocking her kill!

And then it was a moot point. While Emmett obstructed her view, the crack and crunch of breaking bones reached her. She peeked around her mate to see that Levy had snapped the last guy's neck. No coming back from that one. Her inner-*other* pouted at being denied its fun, but retreated nonetheless.

Emmett's hands roamed her body. His warm hands. On her bare skin. Damn it, she'd lost her sheet at some point.

And she was still squishy.

*

Levy surveyed the damage in the suite. They were gonna have a huge fucking bill. He noticed a hole in the bedroom wall that let him see the living room. Huge.

But everyone who mattered was alive. Whitney had a few scratches and Emmett was just as torn to shit as he was, but they were still breathing.

The five wolves in the bedroom were not.

Emmett limped into the living room, Whitney still wrapped in his arms, and he followed behind them. He stepped around debris and settled beside them on the relatively untouched couch.

"That was…" Intense. Horrible. Disgusting. Glorious.

The wolf had howled and rejoiced through the entire battle. It had its mates at its side and flesh beneath his fangs. When Whitney had pulled on them, the *other* responded with glee. She fit them, was part of them in every way.

She was their Warden Born.

"Yeah." Emmett nodded and stroked their mate's bare arm. "We're gonna get shit from the five families." Not that he cared. His wolf felt the need to destroy every one of them.

"Hell, they're going to try and kill us." Whitney chuckled. "Maybe not today, but they will." A growl jumped into his throat before he knew the sound had risen. His mate reached for his hand and twined her fingers with his. "Easy. You didn't see…"

Her eyes grew distant, paling from their beautiful brown and easing to white. "Whitney? Let me see. Let us see."

He wasn't sure she could, didn't know if she even understood what she was able to do. Hell, *he* didn't know what she could do, but he could guess.

Then snapshots assaulted him. Visions of other trios being slaughtered, women decorated in the same swirling Marks as those that covered Whitney were torn to shreds. He recognized the five families represented. A leader from each line present and engaged in the destruction.

Sarvis's memories slipped into him, fed to him by Whitney.

The five families hated humans. They diluted the bloodlines…

So they changed the laws and no single wolves could mate with a human. But that wasn't enough.

They hated the power a human mated to Wardens inherited. The Warden Born took too much, they couldn't be controlled…

So they changed the laws and Warden Born were stricken from memory. The spell was rewritten and they were no longer called to the Gathering.

They hated the idea of a human in a position to lead a pack. They wanted the Alpha Marked gone…

101

And an Alpha Pair destroyed half of the five families. The wolves hadn't done well without their mates.

That law was buried immediately.

If the Elders hadn't been so successful, he would have laughed at the absurdity of their actions.

"You really are ours. Destined. Fated." Levy brought her hand to his face and nuzzled her palm.

"Of course I am. I have the bites, and you know, biological material, to prove it."

Emmett chuckled. "I'll give you biological material, love." His partner leaned down and licked one of Whitney's claiming bites, nipping the tender flesh, and he felt the trembles that overtook her body.

Levy's cock stirred to life. With the end of the fight, he still had adrenaline to burn off, and he couldn't think of a better way to be rid of it than...

"What the fuck a duck?" Scarlet's screech cut through the room like a knife, and he turned to the Alpha Mate with a snarling glare.

The woman didn't even flinch.

She did, however, smile. "I'm gonna get to the destroyed room in a sec, but," she turned her attention to Whitney. "Damn girl, you are one lucky ho."

He felt the draw of energy on his body before he saw the growing glow from his mate. Levy snared a pillow, and plopped it across his lap in a lightning fast movement. "Easy, sweet. No reason to get cranky."

Levy looked to Emmett. Yeah, they'd need to get a cap put on their mate until she learned a little control.

"I'm fine," she snapped and harrumphed. "She was looking at you." Then she turned to Emmett. "And you're naked, too."

Emmett popped from view and immediately returned with a blanket that he tossed across the three of them, blocking their nakedness.

"Bitchy." Scarlet sniffed and then her mates came barreling into the room only to come to a sliding halt.

"What the fuck?" Keller bellowed.

"I asked the same thing." His mate's sister smiled.

Before Madden could jump into the fray as well, Gabriella joined them, her mates in tow, as well. Great, it was a family reunion.

All he'd wanted to do was claim the mate the laws said he couldn't have. Had that been so much to ask? Looking around at the carnage, feeling the aches and pains left over from their fight, he figured it actually had been.

"What the fuck?" Gabby's screech rivaled Scarlet's.

"We asked the same thing. You're third in line. We really should get one of those number systems in here. Like, number 312, ask your question." Scarlet's voice was light, but her worried gaze was centered on Whitney.

Whitney giggled. "You're an idiot."

It was then the tension in the room eased, starting with the eldest Wickham and filtering down through to Gabby's mates.

"Will someone answer my question?" Keller's voice was calm, too calm, so Levy launched into explanations before the Ruling Alpha could decide to take his answers by force.

Silence lasted until the last syllable passed his lips for one beat, then two, then...

"I think Whit has us beat in the bad ass department now." Scarlet turned to Madden and smacked his arm. "How come you didn't give me super powers?"

"I gave you something, baby." The massive Alpha waggled his eyebrows.

Keller simply sighed and closed his eyes, pinching the bridge of his nose while shaking his head.

Emmett leaned close. "They're not taking this seriously."

"Oh," their mate interrupted, her focus on her sisters as they joked and taunted *their* mates. "They are. But the world isn't ending right this second and the Wickhams have never sat around wringing our hands. We'll live life," her gaze turned to them, "share our love, and make plans to take conquer the world over ice cream."

Levy didn't doubt for a second the Wickham triplets would do just that.

Hopefully tomorrow.

For now, he wanted to take his happily ever after and run with it.

THE END

If you enjoyed Whitney, please be totally awesomesauce and leave a review so others may discover it as well. Long review or short, your opinion will help other readers make future purchasing decisions. So, go forth and rate my level-o-awesome!

By the way… you can check at the rest of the Alpha Marked series on Celia's website: http://celiakyle.com/alphamarked

About Celia Kyle

Ex-dance teacher, former accountant and erstwhile collectible doll salesperson, New York Times and USA Today bestselling author Celia Kyle now writes paranormal romances for readers who:

1) Like super hunky heroes (they generally get furry)
2) Dig beautiful women (who have a few more curves than the average lady)
3) Love laughing in (and out of) bed.

It goes without saying that there's always a happily-ever-after for her characters, even if there are a few road bumps along the way.

Today she lives in Central Florida and writes full-time with the support of her loving husband and two finicky cats.

If you'd like to be notified of new releases, special sales, and get FREE eBooks, subscribe here:
http://celiakyle.com/news

You can find Celia online at:
http://celiakyle.com
http://facebook.com/authorceliakyle
http://twitter.com/celiakyle

COPYRIGHT PAGE

Made in the USA
Columbia, SC
08 January 2020